Heiress to her Ma
Bethesda Carfax lea
the smooth-talking f
ton. Determined to
tender age, the wily baronet uses all his accomplish-
ments as a rake to flatter and compromise her.

But his plans are foiled when Bethesda suddenly falls
headlong in love with Marcus, Viscount Mainwaring.
How can she possibly break her rash promise to marry
Sir Maurice? Even for beautiful heiresses, the path of
true love does not run smoothly. And when Bethesda
dramatically runs away from the seemingly insoluble
problem, how can the handsome Viscount reclaim his
beloved heiress?

Runaway Heiress

Alanna Wilson

MILLS & BOON LIMITED
London · Sydney · Toronto

First published in Great Britain 1982
by Mills & Boon Limited, 15-16 Brooks Mews,
London W1A 1DR

ISBN 0 263 74100 1

Set in 10 on 11½pt Linotron Times

04/1282

Photoset by Rowland Phototypesetting Ltd
Bury St Edmunds, Suffolk
Made and printed in Great Britain by
Cox & Wyman Ltd, Reading

CHAPTER
ONE

'I MIGHT have known it—I might have guessed!'

The angry whisper was explosive in the silent drawing-room. A girl stood alone at the window, her bright curls brushing the frame. Her heavy lashes were lowered— her full mouth drooped; now and then she lifted her gaze, but she saw nothing of the pleasant garden outside.

Miss Skeffington's Seminary for Young Ladies, an imposing residence situated in a busy thoroughfare of Brighton, was surrounded by ample grounds, and the noises of the street were far away. A variety of noble trees studded the spacious lawns; late birdsongs trilled in the quiet air. A feeling of dignified refinement permeated the establishment, both outside and within.

To the solitary girl at the window, the drawing-room offered a welcome haven from the happy chatter of the boarders' cosy parlour, where twenty other young ladies of tender years were whiling away the hour before the dressing-bell would ring in comparing excited plans for the approaching Michaelmas holidays. Their ages ranged from eleven to seventeen years, and they were of assorted colouring, stature and intelligence; all, however, had certain things in common. Each one was of impeccable lineage and handsome fortune; and each was eagerly looking forward to the coming week of freedom.

Two or three of the boarders had reached the magic

age of seventeen. For these damsels, the remaining term of the year would mark the end of schooldays; when the Seminary closed its door for the Christmas season the young ladies would return no more; but would face the prospect, when the Yuletide festivities had passed, of being fired off by their respective Mamas into the London season—the yearly Marriage Mart. As for the others, they would be excluded for some time yet from the exciting world of grown-up society; but they could look forward to several days of such holiday delights as the pantomime, visits to Astleys, and private evening parties where they could bask in the reflected glory of elder sisters already 'out'. Anything, it was generally felt, would be a welcome change from the gruelling daily round of drawing lessons, music lessons, dancing lessons, hours on the backboard, and endless reminders of the correct manners and behaviour expected of any young lady so fortunate as to be admitted to the exclusive precincts of Miss Skeffington's.

But the girl staring miserably from the drawing-room window felt no such happy lift of spirits. She saw nothing of the charming vista of well-tended flowerbeds and lawns, where lengthening shadows already marked the close of the golden autumn afternoon.

Bethesda Carfax, sixteen years old, tall, straight and supple, rested her rounded arms on the window-sill and brooded. Those same arms protruded from sleeves that had grown too short. The grey gown and black silk apron worn by all Miss Skeffington's boarders could not hide the straining of a too-tight bodice across her full young breasts. The head of tumbled curls that leaned sadly on the window-frame was of a rich red that glowed warmly even in the shadowy room. Her eyes, long and narrow in a heart-shaped face, were as green as clear water. She was blessed with naturally dark brows and lashes. It gave her some satisfaction, in moments of resentment, to reflect that Amelia had to darken hers.

Bethesda was thinking of her Aunt Amelia now, and with a good deal of bitterness.

Amelia, Lady Carfax, an ethereal beauty accustomed to being much admired, was, Bethesda told herself for the hundredth time, a completely selfish woman. Amelia thought of nothing but the latest fashion in dress, town parties, and gossip. Her entire existence was devoted to pleasure. Her husband, Bethesda's uncle, indulged his frivolous wife endlessly. He was too pleasure-loving and indolent himself, Bethesda thought sadly, to interfere on behalf of his niece—even though she was his own brother's child—banished as a rebellious twelve-year-old to Miss Skeffington's school, and forgotten, it seemed, ever since.

A tear slid from under her lashes, and was angrily dashed away. Always, always the same thing! They will be touring the Continent, or visiting friends, or one of the children is not quite well; always the same!

And now I am not to go home . . . . again.

For it was holiday time, and, once more, a letter had come, containing several plausible-sounding reasons why it would be better if Bethesda did not return to Ansteys. She would be remaining at school for the Michaelmas vacation.

The girl blinked furiously to force back tears, and, staring through the glass, she let her thoughts turn back to the past, and the years of her childhood. She saw herself at twelve years old, a spirited and laughing little girl, an undisputed queen ruling her kingdom of Ansteys. There was no other child in that vast household. Secure, her lightest wish indulged, showered with love from every side, her Mama'a darling, her father's pet, she reigned supreme in a world so perfect that sometimes, looking back, it seemed unreal.

She thought of the day when her tall, handsome, adored Papa, always a reckless whip, had overturned the high-perch phaeton that was really too dangerous to drive with a half-broken team. She remembered her mother, thrown wide into the stone-walled ditch like a broken flower; her father, taken up by the men and carried home, with smashed bones, had lingered for two days before following his wife into the grave. Herself— left suddenly alone.

Alone, to face the awful disbelief of the arrival of Papa's brother, her Uncle Eustace—and Amelia, his wife.

Papa's lawyer, Turvey, had explained it all to her, gently and kindly, but she was frantic with grief and could not take it in. Could not understand that Uncle Eustace now owned Ansteys and all it contained. That the servants, her own dear governess, her beloved nurse Addy who had nursed Mama when she was a little girl, her friend Bolton the head groom—all these were now beholden to her Aunt Amelia, whose orders they must instantly obey. Her world had smashed around her.

She scarcely heard Turvey's compassionate voice, explaining that she herself, however, was not a pauper. On the contrary she was very rich indeed, for her Mama's immense fortune was hers, absolutely; to come into her possession when she was twenty-five, or upon her marriage—whichever was the sooner. She was only aware of the immediate disaster, and overwhelmed by despair and intolerable grief. She thought of the scenes that followed. Her furious refusal of Amelia's authority —her sobs and wild outbursts of rebellion—the inevitable reactions of a sheltered child whose happy world had been shattered forever. The scenes that ended in Amelia branding her a hoyden, uncontrollable and beyond redemption. Her governess was dismissed, her nurse pensioned off, and herself dispatched to Miss Skeffington's, there to remain.

Well, she had learned to hide her feelings, and to comport herself with dignity. But the longing for her beloved home remained. And always, it seemed, as holidays approached, a letter would arrive setting forth the reasons why it would be better if she remained at the school. During the past four years her homecomings had been infrequent indeed. Amelia preferred to reign supreme at Ansteys, the centre of attention, doting on her two pompous little boys, pampered by her husband, enjoying the London seasons as an established beauty. She was not likely to trouble herself with the care of a niece whose looks, as the girl grew into her teens, cast Amelia's own into the shade; and who made an unwanted extra in a household entirely geared to the gratification of the lady's lightest wish.

Long shadows lay across the smooth lawns outside, and darkened beneath the trees. A wave of misery swept over Bethesda, and a sob rose from her breast into her throat.

Her hand flew to her mouth; the drawing-room door opened. She turned, wide-eyed, expecting to confront an outraged Miss Skeffington, demanding an explanation of her presence, without permission, in the drawing-room at that hour.

Instead, a tall gentleman was shown into the room. The door closed softly behind him.

Bethesda stood motionless at the shock of so unexpected a sight. Since her father's death she had never actually been alone with a young man—and a personable young man too, obviously a gentleman of fashion. His blue coat was moulded to his elegant figure, and his pantaloons were of a delicate shade of primrose. His brown hair was pomaded and brushed into a Cherubim, his tasselled topboots gleamed, and two or three tasteful fobs dangled at his waist. His starched shirt-points were so high that he found it rather difficult to turn his head. His coat was padded to give an illusion of breadth to rather narrow shoulders. All in all, he was a startling sight suddenly to appear in the chaste surroundings of Miss Skeffington's maidenly drawing-room.

That his expression was bored and rather sulky, and his fine dark eyes beneath languid lids weary and slightly bloodshot, did not register with Bethesda. A closer observer might also have marked the faint network of lines that was beginning to creep across his face, although his years numbered barely twenty-six. But this, also, escaped her notice.

The rising sob in her throat turned into a gasp of dismay. The blood flamed suddenly under her ivory skin. 'Oh!' she cried, in a rich musical voice, made more appealing by a throaty little catch in its pure tones. 'I must leave—Miss Skeffington will be so vexed!'

Sir Maurice Barrington, advancing across the carpet, halted in mid-step; his attention riveted at the sight that met his eyes. A last slanting sunbeam caught and set afire a dancing red curl; green eyes, polished with unshed tears, gleamed even in the dimness; his practised eye noted with swift appraisal the passionate mouth, the chiselled nose, the sweet determined chin—and took instant and expert note of the long limbs and curving breast and thigh, revealed by that demure, but too-tight gown.

'By God!' he said under his breath, and with narrowed eyes, he stepped across the room, stood before her, and executed a graceful bow.

'Forgive me, ma'am,' he said, in a pleasing, rather light voice. 'I have startled you! Indeed, I did not mean to—and am sorry for it.'

'I—I must not be found here,' she said breathlessly. 'I can slip out by this window—'

'Pray, ma'am, do not leave the room on my account,' he begged politely. 'I have called to see Miss Skeffington, that is all. I have come to escort my sister home for the holidays.'

There was a pause. She stared at him. It was too much; come to escort his sister home for the holidays! The words brought back her misery in a flood. Still staring at him, she bit her lip. The held-back tears welled up; in a moment they would overflow.

'I am Maurice Barrington, at your service,' he said. He was puzzled to see two tears slide down her cheeks from beneath the heavy lashes. There was a short silence; he stood looking at her, slightly at a loss. She struggled for composure, and obedient to the precepts of correct behaviour that had been impressed upon her, though she could see but little through her misted eyes, she swayed smoothly into a curtsey, and managed to find her voice.

'Bethesda Carfax, sir,' she whispered.

'Your obedient servant, Miss Carfax,' he responded,

looking down at her bent head. His jaded senses stirred
as he observed the enchanting half-circle of black satin
lashes that cast shadows on her cheeks. Although he was
not, in general, the kind of man who bestowed much
notice on female agitation, the sight of tears coursing
down the ivory skin awoke in him a faint pang of
sympathy. She was, he realised with practised appreci-
ation, really uncommonly beautiful. Studying her now,
he saw that she was a diamond of the first water; a
dazzler; he could not remember having seen a more
stunning creature. And besides—

Something was stirring in his mind; a faint memory,
becoming clearer—a recollection of something said or
heard—something about the name . . .

'Carfax!' he said suddenly. 'Carfax—you are Miss
Carfax? Why, I remember—Gad, of course! Why, I
know your uncle! You are . . . . You must be . . .'

In the nick of time he stopped himself from complet-
ing the sentence aloud. The words trembled on the tip of
his tongue; but he spoke them only in his brain.

'The Carfax heiress!'

He was galvanised into full attention. He was fairly
well acquainted with Eustace and Amelia Carfax. They
were forever to be met with at the town parties during
the season; he had flirted mildly with Lady Carfax on
several occasions. He had heard of the existence of this
niece. Vaguely he remembered the story. Her parents
killed; the estates, of course, entailed; but a huge fortune, hers outright, safely gathering interest. The figure
danced in his brain—surely, he had heard it mentioned
—eighty thousand a year, at the very least. This girl standing before him was one of England's greatest heiresses.

His mind began to race as he gazed at the wistful face

raised to his own. Eighty thousand a year! Safely invested! Hers absolutely! And as well as that, she was a beauty!

No wonder that Amelia Carfax kept this jewel hidden safely away! Amelia would not relish the attention that such a glowing creature would attract; better to keep her out of sight! But this could not be done forever. Brought out into society the girl must be, and quite soon by the look of her. For if he were any judge—and by God he ought to be—she could be turned sixteen already, perhaps more. And when she emerged from the schoolroom, every gazetted fortune-hunter in town, with his pockets hanging out, would be after her; there was nothing surer that that.

She was looking at him now, faintly questioning. He managed to assemble his wits, and spoke in warm and encouraging tones.

'Why, I know your aunt and uncle well,' he said. 'Indeed, I was at cards with them only last week; we meet forever in town. I feel—permit me to say it, Miss Carfax, I feel as though we are already friends!'

'That is very pleasing, sir,' she replied formally. 'But I must leave now. Miss Skeffington will arrive at any moment. I shall leave by the window, and I would ask you as a favour, sir, not to say that I was here. I shall get into trouble; it is against the rules, you see.'

'I understand,' he responded, 'and indeed I shall say nothing of your presence here. But—forgive me—but I cannot help but see that you are in some distress. Pardon my presumption—but I am, after all, a family friend. Is there not something I can do?'

'No,' she said sadly, turning her face away. 'Thank you, but there is nothing. I bid you good day, sir.'

Her hand was on the catch of the window, to swing it wide. In a moment she would be gone. In the recesses of his brain, a germ of a plan was stirring, faintly, barely formed. He must have time to think it through. But in the meantime it was essential, it was imperative that he should speak to her again. He reached out and laid a tentative hand on her arm.

Startled, grasping the window catch, she turned back to stare at him.

He schooled his voice to low and confiding tones.

'Miss Carfax,' he said, 'I really cannot bear to leave you in such sadness. Remember—I am not a stranger; already, I feel almost in the light of an older brother. Could you not bring yourself to confide in me? If there is any way in which I could be of service to you, I should be so happy!'

He had uttered the one, the only word that could have pierced through the years of schooling in hiding her feelings. That word was 'brother'.

For there had been a brother, once. He had died in childhood, before she was born. But there had been many times, during the past years, when she had wept for him. If he had lived—if he had lived, she would not be standing here, alone, shut out from her own home . . . and he would have been older, perhaps about the age of the young man before her now, who was speaking to her so warmly, so protectively, just as her very own brother would have done; her brother, whom she had never even seen . . .

It was too much. She did not see that the gentle smile on his lips failed to lighten his intent dark eyes, or that he was watching her with a calculating expression, searching for her reaction, ready to vary his approach if necessary. All her pent-up unhappiness swept over her in a giant wave; somehow, she never knew how, her head fell on to his shoulder, placed so invitingly close, and she burst into passionate speech.

'I'm not to go home again!' she sobbed out. 'I am to stay at school—not to go home—it isn't fair! I hate them!'

A masculine arm slid around her shoulders and held her close. A tide of warmth flowed over her, and she rested gratefully on his breast, as trusting as a child, and as vulnerable. He looked down at her gleaming head against his superfine lapel, and his half-formed plan crystallised a little more, became more definite. His heart began to beat faster. What luck—what unbelievable luck! He was a gambler to the core; and now, staking for all or nothing on a single throw, he spoke, urgently, into her ear.

'My dearest child,' he said, 'we cannot talk now; there is no time. But I must—I must help you. I must find out what troubles you so. But you cannot tell me properly now. Listen—I have a plan. Come out into the garden, during the evening and speak to me. I will wait beneath the elm tree, beside the stone bench, near the gate. This evening, dear, whenever you can leave the house unobserved. Will you come?'

With all his senses strained for the moment of Miss Skeffington's imminent approach—for the consequences of being caught here, with the heiress actually nestling in his arms, were dire to contemplate—he stood, rigid with anxiety, and waited for her answer.

A shocked refusal hovered on Bethesda's lips. It was never uttered. The urgency of the moment made it impossible to argue. Years of correct decorum, instilled by the unremitting efforts of Miss Skeffington and her satellites, fought briefly with the passionate need to pour out all her wrongs and hurt feelings to this sympathetic listener—and lost. She heard herself say words that sounded incredible in her own ears.

'If you would wait until everyone is asleep, I—I could slip out through this window,' she whispered. 'But it will be late—midnight, perhaps!'

Excitement began to rise in his heart. Certain snubs dealt him by the fashionable Carfax set might—just might—be about to be repaid, with ample interest. 'I will stand beneath the elm, by the side gate, until you come.' Wise in the ways of assignations, he did not say how long he would wait. The knowledge that he was standing out there in the darkness, perhaps until dawn, might serve to bring her out of the house, even though he knew that in the intervening hours her courage would probably begin to ebb.

'The gate—it will be locked,' she breathed.

'Leave that to me,' he said firmly. He lifted her hand, bending his head to kiss her palm. 'Now, little friend, you must leave. Can you escape from here without being discovered?'

'Yes—if you will close this window after me,' she answered, and suddenly smiled, revealing an enchanting dimple beside her mouth. 'I shall run along the terrace, go in at the side door, and gain my own room.'

'*Au revoir*, then!' and he pressed her fingers warmly. 'Until this evening—do not let me wait in vain!'

'I won't,' she cried breathlessly. She stepped through the window. He replaced the catch, and was apparently admiring the prospect through the glass, when the door opened and Miss Skeffington, severely modish in rustling black silk and rimless eyeglasses, entered the room; with graceful apologies on her lips for having unavoidably kept dear Miss Barrington's brother waiting.

As he explained to the lady that the sudden illness of the maiden aunt whose usual task it was had made it necessary for her brother to escort Melinda home for the holidays, and bowed himself out with all the aplomb of one accustomed from childhood to move in the first social circles, his pulses were beating with a rising excitement. Urbanely smiling, he assured Miss Skeffington that he would present himself the following morning ready to undertake the journey home to Suffolk. As he spoke smilingly, with well-bred courtesy and ease of manner, the headmistress would have been astounded if she could have read the thoughts seething behind his respectful face. She would have been even more amazed had she been privileged to see him, slumped ugly-drunk in some pothouse in the London slums, rubbing elbows with whores and thieves, seeking further thrills to stimulate his weary senses—or if she had known of the succession of light ladies, as lovely as they were ruthless, who had helped him to dissipate the very handsome fortune which had been his upon the death of his father. As he left Miss Skeffington with a suitably affectionate message for his sister—a lumpy brat of thirteen who irritated him with her chatter—he reflected once again on the damned thoughtlessness of his late unlamented father, who had tied up Melinda's lavish dowry all right and tight, so that her hapless brother could not dip his fingers into it when his luck was down.

However—fortune might be about to smile upon him now, and in a most unexpected way. He accepted his

curly-brimmed beaver and his amber cane from a deferential housemaid; the front door was opened for him;
and he departed into the late autumn afternoon, a
benign expression on his face, and hope singing in his
heart.

Bethesda, meanwhile, hearing the latch click to behind her, gathered up her skirts and ran swiftly along the
length of the terrace, where among the tall manicured
shrubs darkness was already gathering. She rounded the
western corner of the house, to the side door which was
still unbolted; it would be fastened when the clock struck
five. She glided up the stairs, along two corridors, up a
flight of narrower stairs; and so gained the safety of her
bedroom, at the same moment as the sound of the
dressing-bell rang through the house.

In a few minutes the other boarders would make their
way upstairs, still whispering and giggling, to change
their gowns for dinner. Bethesda pressed the palms of
her hands to her flushed face. The enormity of what she
had promised—a secret meeting with a young man at
night—shook her from head to foot. The consequences
of discovery were too awful to imagine. She drew a deep
breath, lifted her chin, and stiffened her resolution.
After all—he was not a stranger; he was acquainted with
her family; he was Melinda's brother. She felt certain of
his kindness, his warmth and understanding. She was
hungry for comfort; and the touch of a masculine hand,
strong and sympathetic, seemed to linger on her own.
Papa had used to hold her hand in his, when they walked
together, back in that childhood world—holding her
fingers in his strong slim ones, as they wandered in the
garden, or visited the stables, or the greenhouses. She
had often rested her head on Papa's shoulder, when she

was tired, or just when she wanted to be close to him.
And—if her own brother had not died . . .

Her mind was made up. She would not fail.

Evening prayers had been said, and the young ladies
took up their candles, one by one, and made their way
upstairs to their respective bedrooms. Bethesda thanked
heaven that the dignity of her sixteenth birthday had
brought with it the privilege of a room of her own. She
climbed into the white-curtained four-poster, and,
quivering with suppressed emotion, she forced herself to
lie still under the covers, breathing deeply, eyes closed.
The door opened, and Matron, candle in hand, looked
in as she made her last round of boarders' rooms.
Shaking with mixed fear and excitement, Bethesda lay,
as silence gradually settled over the house.

At last, all seemed still. Carefully, she pushed the
blankets back and reached in the dark for the serviceable
drab cloak worn by all the boarders when outdoors. She
found her slippers and groped for the door. Softly, with
caught breath, she opened it; a dim light burned in the
deserted passage. On tip-toe, she stole past the row of
shut doors. On the half-landing of the stairs, another
night-light gave out a faint glow. She glided down the
stairs and across the wide hall. The drawing-room was
closed, but the door, well-oiled by Miss Skeffington's
diligent housemaids, made no sound as she pushed it
open. She flitted across the carpet to the long windows.
The catch was loose and made no noise under her
trembling fingers. She stopped long enough to thrust her
handkerchief, folded into a wedge, between frame and
sill, so that the window might not swing shut behind her,
locking her out. Then she was clear of the house.

She flew across the terrace; and ran full speed, gasping with fright and excitement, through the dark profusion of shrubs; across the shadowed lawns; skirting the avenue of trees that fringed the gravelled driveway. Still running, she came, swift as a swallow, to the place where Barrington stood, muffled to the ears in a many-caped driving coat. Her rush carried her straight towards him; and as she drew near, his arms opened instantly to receive her. The next moment she was caught in his embrace—knee to knee and breast to breast, the heavy folds of his coat around them both, her eyes, luminous even in the dimness, staring wildly, half-blindly into his.

Barrington could not believe his good luck.

He had expected anything—tears, hesitancy, angry reproaches for making her take so fearful a risk; even that she might not come at all. Her long legs were pressed against his own. His arms were clasped around a firm yet supple waist. He could actually feel the waves of emotion shuddering through her body, and the desperate heaving of her breast against his own.

With a sure gambler's instinct for when the cards were about to fall his way, he realised that it was now or never.

He bent his lips towards her ear; and spoke in a low throbbing whisper.

'I love you,' he said, and his listening ears approved the passionate tremor of his own voice. 'I love you. Will you be my wife?'

His words hit her like a thunderbolt. Bereft of speech, she stared up at him; her mouth worked, her lips moved, but no sound came.

He tightened his arms around her.

'I have frightened you,' he said tenderly. 'But how could I help it? From the moment I saw you, I knew. My heart left my bosom then, and flew to you.' He paused, searching her face. She gazed dumbfounded at him still, her lips parted. But she made no move to withdraw from his embrace. Encouraged, he persevered.

'As my wife, you would be valued as you should be,' he said in caressing tones. 'My only thought would be for your happiness. Every comfort and elegance of life would be yours. Secure in the status of marriage, your every wish would be indulged.' Yes, he thought, with a sudden gleam of amusement, I can certainly promise you every comfort, since with your fortune at my command, there will be plenty for all my needs, and even enough for yours. We will both have all that money can buy—and I will not even interfere with your pleasures, my dear, unless you try to interfere with mine.

If only he could wring a promise from her, and perhaps a token to bind her to her word, then he would be able to stave off his most pressing creditors. A hint dropped here and there of his forthcoming marriage to the Carfax heiress would restore his credit—keep him afloat, at least for the immediate future.

For marriage it must be. His carriage was outside the gates, and his henchman waiting. It would be a simple matter to carry her off here and now, and make for Gretna Green. But long before they reached the Scottish border, he would be intercepted; and prison awaited the abductor of an heiress. The money was out of her reach, in any case, unless she married him. So marry him she must. He stood, rigid with anxiety, his eyes fixed on her own.

'Will you honour me?' he asked urgently. 'Will you make me the happiest of men?'

Had he flushed the bird too soon? Had his words

sounded false—rehearsed? Was the game lost?

But again luck was with him. For he had been fortunate enough to hit on the one thing that was most likely to weigh with her, in the state of repressed emotion that she had been in all through that long day.

The words were singing through her brain.

'Secure in the status of marriage!'

Secure—safe—free from Amelia—free to do as she pleased; never again to bow to her stepmother's will, or suffer her petty malices, her spite! Secure in the status of marriage.

Under the shadow of his hat brim, his eyes were fixed on hers. He was waiting, pleading for an answer. His arms around her body were strong, warm, reassuring. She drew a deep breath.

'Yes, oh yes!' she cried out. 'I will marry you, I will!'

She buried her face in his shoulder and burst into overwrought sobs.

Holding her close. Barrington stroked her hair gently, murmuring endearments in her ears. But as she continued to weep, his encircling arms gradually relaxed. Her wet face was ruining his cravat; and besides, it was damned cold to be standing still in the sharp wind that fluttered the autumn leaves along the paths, billowing the skirts of his riding coat, and reminding him that his feet were damp from the heavy dew. Bethesda did not notice a faint note of impatience, instantly suppressed, as he said.

'Love, let us sit down together here, on this bench. We will talk quietly about what it is that upsets you so.'

He settled her gently on the rustic seat, wrapping the folds of his voluminous coat around them both with studied care. He hoped that she did not often fall into hysterical fits. Although he carefully cultivated an air of smiling good humour, he was not by nature an even-tempered man. Any display of emotion on the part of females with their silly vapours tended to spark off the suppressed irritability of his own temperament. But he must be careful not to offend her; the bargain had yet to be sealed.

Bethesda grew gradually quiet. A feeling of peace was stealing over her, the natural aftermath of an emotional storm. Here, in this secluded place, leaning on his arm, sheltered by his coat, she felt that she could stay forever. She nestled closer and relaxed against his chest. He eased his arm and shoulder slightly; she was dazzling, by gad, but no fragile beauty. He said, hoping to bring her to a more rational frame of mind,

'Why are you not going home for the holidays, my love?'

'Aunt Amelia wrote that I am not to go,' she answered dreamily. It did not seem to matter so much now. She went on, 'I had received an invitation to spend the holidays in London, with Lady Cumnor. Lady Cumnor is the mother of Constance, my best friend. And in a postscript to her letter, my aunt gave permission for me to accept the invitation. But—but I cannot go to London either.'

'You cannot go to London either? Why not?'

'I haven't any suitable gowns,' she said, and her lip trembled. 'I have not had any new clothes for months— Aunt Amelia always forgets to send my allowance, and I have not any money left at all—not even for vails for the servants. I should be ashamed; I'd much rather not go at all.'

An idea, faint but brilliant, was sparked off in his

fertile brain.

'What would you need?' he asked. 'You would not go out to evening parties, of course. You would be with the schoolroom party; Lady Cumnor has several younger children, I believe.'

'No, of course—we wouldn't go to balls or parties. Constance is only fifteen. But we would go to see the sights, and walk in the park, and to the drawing-room after dinner. I should so enjoy it. I have not been to London since—since I was sent to school.' Her voice quivered. 'But it's no use. Even my white evening dress is much too small. But why do I speak of it? There is nothing to be done.'

'As to that,' he said, with a quick smile, 'I think there is something to be done. What would you say if, tomorrow, some dress-boxes arrived, ostensibly from your aunt? I know of a skilled modiste, here in Brighton, who would certainly know just what would be correct for your needs, and who would happily supply it.'

Delighted, incredulous, she looked up; the colour rose under her clear skin. Her eyes sparkled—then as suddenly clouded; her face fell.

'But—I have no money,' she said. 'I can't get any of my money. Not until I am twenty-five, or until I am married.'

'But you are going to be married,' he pointed out. 'And since that is so, it is perfectly proper for me to make you a gift.' And in expectation of a rich return I make it, he added silently. For the idea that had come to him was an inspiration indeed. If he could persuade her to accept clothes that he had paid for, and actually to wear those clothes in the house of Lady Cumnor, she would be socially damned. The scandal of such improper behaviour, if it were ever known, would blacken her reputation forever. Should she be tempted to go back on her promise to marry him, the threat of exposure of her conduct would surely bring her to heel. And if, by some miracle, he could also cozen her into writing him a letter . . .

She was looking at him now, trusting him, but still with doubt in her eyes.

'As my affianced bride, you may accept from me whatever you choose,' he said with easy assurance. 'I have no ring for you; so will you not accept this instead, until I can make you a proper betrothal gift? Besides—' he leaned closer; she was wavering; he could sense it—'besides, nobody will know. It will be our secret, our very own. Something to laugh over together when we are married.'

'When we are married,' she said, with something of wonder in her voice. 'Yes—I do see that. It is quite proper—now that you explain it so—you are truly sure?'

'Quite sure,' he said, with concealed satisfaction. 'All that you require for your week of pleasure will arrive on the morrow. And now—' he rose, and drew her to her feet, taking both her hands. 'Now, you must return to the house. It is dangerous to stay here too long. Is your room on this side?'

'Yes.'

'When you are safely there, wave a handkerchief from the window. Then I shall know that all is well. And now goodnight, my darling.'

'Goodnight,' she said, in a shy whisper.

'Will you do just one little thing for me?' he asked caressingly.

'Of course,' she answered, and once more the dimple

showed beside her mouth. She was certainly a diamond, he reflected, and her looks alone would make him the envy of the town. And then—that wealth! Well, she should be free to have her little affairs, as long as she was discreet. He did not mean to be actively unkind to her. A rosy vista of happy affluence, with unlimited funds to draw on for his indulgence, stretched gloriously before him. He clasped her hands warmly in his own.

'Will you give me, as a keepsake, this little ring you wear?' he asked. Before she could reply, he had slipped it from her hand. 'See—it just fits my smallest finger. I will wear it always, my love.'

The ring had been hers since childhood. It had belonged to her mother. Had she been less emotionally spent, she would have cried out in protest. But it seemed, under the circumstances, ungenerous to do so. He had been so kind; he was her future husband. A faint remonstrance hovered on her lips, but he gave her no chance to speak.

'Tomorrow, when your gowns arrive, write a note to me,' he said. 'Tell me if they are just what you require. Place the note here—in the fork of this tree. The gatekeeper will get it to me. I have bribed him.' He laughed gently at the surprise on her face. 'How did you think I got in here tonight, little innocent? Now—' he took her arm, and guided her hand into a hollow place, well hidden from sight in the old tree. 'If you wish to reach me at any time, place your missive here. The gatekeeper will see that I receive it.' He lifted her hand to his lips, and turned her in the direction of the darkened house. 'Now you must not say another word, or stay here another moment.' He gave her a little push. 'Goodnight, my darling; remember—wave your handkerchief when you are safe.'

He stood among the rustle of falling leaves and watched her receding figure melt into the shadows. He stood waiting, until he saw, high on the third floor of the house, a flutter of white against a black rectangle of window. He gave a soundless whistle of relief; and, with jubilation in his heart, he made his way swiftly and silently to the garden gate that had been left unfastened by the obliging—and well-paid—gatekeeper. A short way along the street, his curricle waited, with side lamps dimmed and a yawning groom holding the horses. Barrington drew out his watch. It was half an hour after midnight. Not too late to arouse Celestine, presumably sleeping in her luxurious rooms, above her equally luxurious dressmaking establishment in the main street. Celestine might not be pleased at being disturbed; but that could not be helped. Damnit, she had enjoyed enough of his patronage in the past—spent on the backs of the various birds of paradise who had helped him to squander his inheritance. It would be an amusing change for Celestine to supply at his request a set of chaste and virginal garments suitable for a schoolgirl not yet out.

As he swung up to the driving seat and gathered the reins hurrying thoughts whirled through his brain. He felt certain the game was his. The girl's own ring was on his finger. He was convinced that she would write him a grateful letter. He grinned at the thought. And there was more. The silly pea-goose was about to visit the house of Lady Cumnor—a matron of impeccable social rectitude, and bosom-friends with half the patronesses of Almack's —actually displaying gowns and other fripperies that he, Barrington, had paid for. Nothing could ever restore the good name of a girl guilty of such shocking conduct, if it ever became known.

As the horses clopped through the streets his mind worked on. Once again, he briefly considered an elopement, but dismissed the idea with regret. The girl was under age—they would have to make for Gretna Green; and long before they got there, the Carfax minions would catch up with him. And then there would be only one sure destination for him; Newgate prison.

No, she must marry him openly, and with Carfax's permission. He was tolerated barely by the Carfax set; his encounters with them were confined to card-parties and masquerades; he had never dined in their house. Carfax would be furious—he would be outraged—at the prospect of such a marriage. But he would have to agree and make the best of it, at least in public. For he would know that if Barrington chose to open his mouth the girl would be disgraced in the eyes of the ton, labelled a wanton; fast; she would be ostracised by polite society; the resulting scandal would rock the whole family to its foundations. The girl's downfall would discredit them all; she would never make a respectable marriage. His grin deepened to show sharp white teeth in the dim light. Oh, no, Carfax could rage and storm as he pleased. He would be forced to bestow the heiress on Maurice Barrington; and with a good grace too.

For the present, however, the clever thing to do was to wait a little. The girl must soon be brought out of seclusion and launched upon the marriage market. And then—then, he, Barrington, would make his move.

The curricle drew up before a darkened doorway. He jumped lightly down from the box, ran up the steps, and began to beat a lively tattoo upon the closed and shuttered entrance of Celestine's.

CHAPTER
TWO

BETHESDA closed the bedroom window, climbed into her bed, pulled up the covers and almost immediately sank into a profound and dreamless sleep; a sleep born of the aftermath of pent-up feeling, long suppressed and at last released. A watcher might have thought her unconscious, so still she lay, one arm outflung; her hair, unbraided, tumbed in curls over the pillows. She was still deeply asleep when the morning bell for the boarders to rise rang through the house. She got up, dressed, assembled with the others for morning prayers. She breakfasted and made her way to the schoolroom for lessons all in a dreamlike state, scarcely aware of her surroundings. She had never been a chatterbox and the other girls, remembering that she was not to go home for the holidays, put her abstraction down to sadness; and saw nothing amiss.

As they filed along the corridor that led to the schoolroom, Bethesda felt a small hand slipped into her own. She looked down into the face of Constance, her dearest friend among the boarders. Constance stood little higher than Bethesda's shoulder; they loved each other dearly, but their relationship was that of older and younger sister rather than equals. Bethesda was so tall, so womanly, that she seemed grown-up in Constance's eyes, and though she adored her friend, the younger girl

was just a little in awe of her. Bethesda returned the
gentle pressure of Constance's fingers, and smiled down
into the sweet face, with its clear blue eyes, looking just
now rather anxiously into her own. She was deeply fond
of the other girl, but she could not, in this particular
matter, see Constance as a confidante. It would be like
confiding in a child—a gentle, true, loving child—but
still a child. Constance would be both worried and
shocked by Bethesda's enormous secret. And besides—
somehow, she could not imagine herself speaking about
it to anyone, no matter how close; not just at present.
Only to herself did she admit the truth; the truth that the
midnight meeting in the garden—her promise to marry
—the incredible fact that she was now betrothed,
seemed totally unbelievable.

In the ordered atmosphere of morning lessons, in the
firmly scholastic surroundings of the rather spartan
schoolroom, the events of the night before seemed,
more than anything else, like a wildly improbable
dream.

She felt the empty place on her finger where Mama's
gold ring had rested for so many years. A tiny trickle of
uneasiness ran through her veins. No, it had certainly
not been a dream. And—to be sure, she had no regrets,
and would do just the same again. Only . . . she did not
object, of course, to giving him a keepsake; he was, after
all, her promised husband! But . . . a thought rose to the
surface, and persisted.

I did not give him Mama's ring. He took it.

I would have given it to him—of course; but I wish—I
wish he had waited until I said he might have it.

She tried to paint in her mind a clear picture of his
face. She could not do so. The light in the drawing-room

had been dim, and their meeting very brief; last night, in the garden, the brim of his hat had almost obscured his face. She could recall only a clean-shaven chin, a thin mouth, a glimpse of brown hair. With some effort she conjured up a memory of his eyes—they were brown, she thought; but thinking back, she could not seem to read into them any particular expression.

However, she was able clearly to recall his voice, anxiously pleading and tender, and to feel his strong encircling arms. And so she tried, with resolution, to thrust aside a faint cold fear that she had too hastily committed her future into the hands of an unknown. But in spite of her efforts, the small worried inner voice remained; it accompanied her through the rest of the day, and hovered on the edge of her mind as she slept, and rose with her in the morning; all her determination could not quite suppress the tinge of nagging unease.

These tiresome and niggling qualms were scattered and put to flight, however, when after luncheon on the second day Miss Skeffington herself entered the boarders' parlour, to bring Miss Carfax the happy news. With a kindly smile, she informed Bethesda that several large dress-boxes, bearing on their pink and silver lids the name of an elegant modiste, had been delivered to the Seminary. All doubts melted in a surge of delight. The servant bringing the boxes had also been the bearer of a polite note from Celestine. This stated that the order had been bespoken through the post by Lady Carfax, in anticipation of the coming visit of her niece to London, for the duration of the holiday.

Blushing guiltily at this blatant deception, Bethesda sprang to her feet. Accompanied by envious looks from the other young ladies—for not until one's come-out did one have gowns from so expensive a modiste as Celestine—she had followed in Miss Skeffington's wake, as that lady led the way in stately fashion to Bethesda's room. And when they arrived, there indeed, laid out upon the bed, were several boxes—be-ribboned and frivolous—and awaiting her attention. Flushed with excitement, she turned on impulse to the schoolmistress.

'Oh, how lovely!' she cried. 'May I open them now? Oh, Miss Skeffington—now I can go to London!'

A timely reproof at such unbridled display of pleasure, unbecoming to the grave composure of a well-bred maiden, rose to Miss Skeffington's lips; but she was fond of Bethesda, her rather grim mouth relaxed. Privately, she considered that the girl was not valued as she should be. Amelia Carfax was well known to the schoolmistress. Amelia herself had been educated at the Seminary as a parlour-boarder, and Miss Skeffington had always considered her a selfish nit-wit. She knew of no reason to alter her opinion. Lady Carfax was in no way a suitable person to have the care and upbringing of a growing girl. Bethesda was better off, the lady considered, under the seminary roof. But that did not excuse her aunt's neglect; Miss Skeffington could not condone the lengthy banishment of the child from her home. She was, in fact, rather surprised at this belated gesture of generosity from Bethesda's aunt, but on reflection, concluded that Amelia had always been an arrant snob; and had doubtless been unwilling to offend so influential a figure as Lady Cumnor by refusing her flattering invitation that Bethesda should be her guest. Graciously, she acceded to the girl's request.

'Certainly, you may open the boxes now. And, since your aunt must have ordered by guess, it is possible that some slight alterations may have to be made to the gowns, to fit your figure. Mamselle is clever with her needle, and I have arranged for her to be excused from classes for the rest of the day. Between the two of you, you must manage; Lady Cumnor's carriage calls for Lady Constance tomorrow morning; you will have to be ready to travel by then.'

'How kind you are!' Bethseda exclaimed, in real gratitude. She stretched a hand towards the silver bow that topped the largest box, and paused. 'Ma'am, please may Constance help me open them? I should like that so much.'

'Very well. I shall send her to you,' said the lady, with an indulgent smile. She departed in a rustle of mulberry silk. Before many minutes had passed, the door opened and the smiling face of Constance appeared. Bethesda caught her by the hand, and the two stood side by side, looking at the tinselled packages waiting on the bed. Then with one accord, red curls mingling with soft brown ringlets, they fell upon those tantalising silver bows.

Then followed an interval of feminine delight, as the boxes were opened, their contents taken out, exclaimed over, laid out on the counterpane and the chest of drawers. Drifts of silver tissue paper floated unheeded to the carpet. Celestine, considerably tickled by the novelty of supplying a rake like Barrington with a set of garments for a maiden still in the schoolroom, had truly excelled herself. There were three dresses, all impeccably correct and in exquisite taste. There was a walking dress of deep amber, highly becoming to Bethesda's rich colouring; a moss-green travelling costume, plain and elegant, fashioned by a master-hand; and delicate white

muslin, lace-trimmed and demure, for the evenings.
There was a set of dainty India muslin underwear that
would defy the scrutiny of the most high-nosed lady's
maid. Bethesda was too happy even to blush at its
sheerness when held against the light. There were smart
half-boots of kid, and a pair of white satin sandals for
evening wear. And to cap it all, from the bottom of the
last dress-box came a flat blue velvet case, which, when
opened, revealed a short but pretty string of seed pearls.

'Bethy,' Constance said, surprised. 'Has Lady Carfax
given you back your Mama's pearls?'

Hot tears rose to Bethesda's eyes. How had he
known? Among her Mama's jewels, locked away in her
case, was a certain small string of pearls, not large, but
lustrous and perfectly matched. They had been her
mother's as a child, and tenderly bestowed upon the
small Bethesda when she was four years old. She had
worn them constantly throughout her childhood. Worn
them, that is, until Amelia had taken them away from
her, to put away, she said, with her Mama's other
jewellery. She had begged to keep the little string;
Mama had meant her to wear them. But Amelia was
adamant. A schoolgirl had no need of any jewels, she
informed her niece. They were quite unnecessary.

And somehow—by some almost unbelievable insight
—he had guessed what would most please her. He had
sent her these, to take the place of her own.

'No,' she said unsteadily. 'No—these are not Mama's.
But—they are very pretty.' All her uneasy doubts and
the vague anxiety that had teased her mind during the
past hours ebbed away. A person capable of such intuit-
ive kindness must be, indeed, most truly the gentleman.
He was, after all, exactly what he seemed—a true and

tender friend, who had divined just exactly what she would like, and what would make her happy. She felt guilty, conscience-stricken, at having even momentarily begrudged him her Mama's ring.

But how had he known?

Actually, he had not known. He had turned back on Celestine's doorstep, the night before, and pulled from the deep pocket of his coat the slim little velvet case. It had been thrown at his head, together with a diamond-heeled shoe, by a certain dazzling light of love with whom he had had a brief encounter, before juicier prey had moved into her orbit. 'Take your cheap trumpery and get out!' she besought him, in pure Cockney tones. 'I ain't wasting my time—down and out, is what you are!' Her words had rung uncomfortably true in his ears. He was, if not down and out, dangerously close to that unhappy state. The size of the payment demanded by Celestine had cost him a severe qualm. But, after all, when angling for a prime fish, it was necessary to use a tempting bait. Pausing on the threshold of the dress-maker's, he said, 'Here—put this in with the rest of it,' and tossed her the case. Celestine, examining its contents, felt a transient pang of sympathy for the unknown innocent—only a schoolroom miss, judging from his instructions—who was fool enough to swim into Barrington's net. Then, closing and bolting the door, she retired upstairs to her interrupted sleep, shrugging her shoulders; it was none of her business.

With the help of Mamselle's nimble fingers, the gowns were made ready to wear in a very short time. Actually, to Mamselle's surprise, little was required in the way of alteration. A hem slightly shortened here—a tiny tuck in a waistband there—it was soon done. Lady Carfax, thought Mamselle, had judged her niece's size with astonishing accuracy, considering that she had not seen Miss Carfax for many months. But still—a lady of fashion, such as Bethesda's aunt, was doubtless supremely skilled in all matters of *la toilette*; that would explain it, perhaps. And her taste—exquisite! Mamselle made a tiny *moue* of approval as she held up the muslin gown. So correct, yet so chic. Even the evening slippers and the half-boots fitted to perfection, after the addition of a little cotton wadding in the toes. Sir Maurice, who had so expertly assessed the exact shape of his betrothed's figure, had slightly over-estimated the size of Bethesda's feet.

By the time Mamselle had departed the afternoon was well advanced. A bare half-hour remained before the dressing-bell. Left alone in the privacy of her bedroom, Bethesda thought quickly. Constance was in the music-room, occupied with her practice on the pianoforte. With luck, no-one else would come in. For there was a letter to be written and safely placed in the hollow elm; and no time to be lost. She balanced the ink-bottle dangerously on the counterpane, and, writing tablet on her knee, and one eye on the door, she dashed off in haste an impulsive missive which—when it found its way into Barrington's hands—was destined to exceed even his wildest expectations.

'My dearest Sir Maurice,' wrote Bethesda, 'how can I thank you for your Great Kindness to me? How clever of you to say that the gowns were from my Aunt! She will never find out, and it will be our own precious Secret, to laugh over when we are Married. The dresses are just exactly what I needed, and everything is in Exquisite taste. I shall be properly clothed down to my very Skin!

How bold I sound, dearest Sir, but you are my Betrothed and wear my ring. I am so happy to receive the pearls, and accept them as a Betrothal Gift, with deepest Thanks and a Heart overflowing with Gratitude. Ever yours, Bethesda Carfax.'

'Lady Constance, the gentlemen have entered the drawing-room,' said Nurse. She bustled into the warm bedroom, with its leaping fire and multitude of candles. 'Are you ready to go down, young ladies? Let me look at you.'

Surveying the two as they stood side by side, Nurse reflected that the Carfax girl would probably make her come-out a full season before Constance. That was just as well! She loved her nursling dearly, and bestowed unqualified approval on Constance's looks; the soft brown hair had been prettily arranged by Lady Cumnor's maid, and the sprigged muslin gown and blue sash were highly becoming to her blue eyes and wild-rose complexion.

But it had to be admitted that the glowing creature standing next to Constance completely cast her darling into the shade. Just the kind of looks, Nurse thought, to take a man's eye . . . The sort that stood out among the yearly crop of debutantes fresh from the schoolroom, making all the others look insipid. And there was all that money as well . . . It was fortunate that the girl was sure of being wed in her first season, before Constance was launched on the marriage mart. Miss Carfax would be snapped up instantly . . .

'Who is in the drawing-room, Nurse?' Constance enquired.

'Just Lady Julia and Sir John, love,' was the reply, 'and Her Grace, who arrived from Andover this morn-

ing. Your brother is expected hourly, however; Turner
arrived with the luggage a few minutes ago. His
Lordship has stopped to dine, but should arrive in time
to join the party. You may see him in the drawing-room
this evening.'

'Oh!' cried Constance in delight. 'Bethy, did you
hear? Marcus is soon to arrive! Let us go down; he may
even be here already!'

On the broad landing above the main staircase the rest
of the schoolroom party was assembled. Lady Caroline,
a pert twelve-year-old, soon to join her sister Constance
at Miss Skeffington's, and Lady Diana, a dimpled pop-
pet of eight years, were standing with Miss Hartigan, the
family governess. The Honourable Rupert, a stout cher-
ub of five, was judged too young to join the company
downstairs; and would remain in Nurse's charge, to hear
a bedtime story on her comfortable lap before the fire.

Side by side Bethesda and Constance began to descend the staircase. The Ladies Caroline and Diana
followed, under the sharp eye of Miss Hartigan, who
brought up the rear of the party. Lit by many candles in
gilded wall-sconces, the huge stairs curved down
gracefully to a spacious hall, where leaping flames
blazed in a marble fireplace, very large and ornately
carved. Bethesda, her hand linked in Constance's, gave
a happy little sigh.

The past few days had been the most pleasant that she
had experienced for a long time. Lady Cumnor, stately,
rather grave of face, had nevertheless treated her with
the greatest kindness. She had known Bethesda's
Mama, and held her memory in deep affection. She
privately thought it a great pity that tragic circumstances
had committed a young girl into so careless a pair of

hands as Amelia Carfax's. Lady Cumnor was acquainted with Amelia, naturally, but they seldom met. The frivolous set of smart young matrons and pseudo-Corinthian dandies who constituted the Carfax set did not appeal to the Countess. Secure in the possession of name, birth, and vast estates, Lady Cumnor deplored the thoughtless conduct of those dashing high-born ladies who startled the town with their spirited exploits, damping their petticoats to make them cling, driving fast curricles in the park, and losing large sums of money at their never-ending card parties. It would be a pity, thought the Countess, if this beautiful child should emerge from the schoolroom, only to fall into the unsuitable ways of Amelia and her cronies. Bethesda's salvation, reflected the motherly lady, would be to speedily attach a husband, wise, kind, and protective. It would be unfortunate if the girl were to succumb to the wiles of some unscrupulous fortune-hunter; for certainly Lady Carfax was too feather-brained to warn or guide her.

Descending the length of the broad thick-carpeted stairs, Bethesda thought with pleasure of the past few days; the sights revisited—Astley's daring equestriennes, the vast and awe-inspiring Museum, the Abbey, the Tower. It was like re-living the happy times of her childhood. Constance had taken delight in sharing Bethesda's enjoyment. They had visited the gardens at Kew, and partaken of ices at Gunter's, all under the benevolent eye of Miss Hartigan, who had derived real satisfaction from escorting so appreciative a pair on a round of innocent pleasures. The girls' enjoyment was so eager and spontaneous that the governess, though she was normally quiet and reserved, could not remain aloof. Charles, the third footman, dutifully following in the wake of the three ladies, heard their laughter and allowed his dignified expression to relax a little. This young lady was a nice friend for their little ladyship to have, he reflected tolerantly. Bring Lady Constance out of herself a bit; he had sometimes thought that she was a bit overlooked, like, though when His Lordship was at home he took her about and made much of her. Great friends, them two, especially for brother and sister. Anyway, thought Charles, looking benignly down his nose from his impressive height of six foot three, it was nice to see the morts having a bit of fun—even the old dragon.

The schoolroom party had rounded the curve of the staircase. They had almost reached the bottom of the long flight.

'Oh, Bethy! Pray that Marcus comes home tonight!' breathed Constance, and her fingers trembled slightly in Bethesda's.

'I am sure he will, love,' answered her friend, smiling in sympathy at the delicately flushed face upturned to her own. Bethesda had been hearing about this marvellous brother all the week. His praises had been constantly sung by the entire family. Marcus, Viscount Mainwaring, scion of the house of Cumnor—heir to the Earldom; twenty-three years old, his mother's darling, his father's pride; adored by the entire household. The best, the dearest, the most wonderful of all possible big brothers, said Constance, her face glowing with eagerness. He was so handsome, so charming, that half of the ladies in London were madly in love with him. A noted sportsman and rider; a non-pareil behind a spirited team; equally at home in the ballroom or on the hunting-field. But, Constance explained, it wasn't really these attributes that made Marcus so splendid. No; it was because, be he never so busy with social engagements, he always had time for his young sisters and brother. When he was at home, he would take Constance driving with him—and had already taught her to handle the ribbons. He was never too high in the instep to come and share nursery tea, playing at soldiers on the carpet with Rupert, or drawing them all, including Nurse, into some hilarious game or other. Why, Constance vividly remembered one night when she was only nine years old, and miserable with a cold, Marcus had cried off from attending an evening party, and had spent the whole time at her bedside, coaxing her to drink soothing draughts, and telling her stories to settle her to sleep.

No, said Constance fervently to her friend, there never was such a brother! She only hoped that when he married—as some day he must—he would fall in love with a girl both beautiful and good, as he deserved.

Bethesda had listened to all of this with a sympathetic smile; but secretly she had grown a little tired of hearing about this marvellous paragon. One's ears did grow dulled by repetition. And surely one reputedly so perfect, so apparently endowed with every masculine virtue, must also be in actual fact a trifle boring? She felt certain that the Viscount was no doubt an extremely worthy young man. But she felt sure that he would never on any account do anything so romantic, so dashing, as making a secret assignation with a young lady still in the schoolroom, or proposing marriage to her after only one meeting.

Going down the stairs, hand-in-hand with Constance, Bethesda's smile deepened at this thought. Her foot touched the bottom tread.

Constance's hand suddenly slid from her clasp. Disregarding Miss Hartigan's restraining cluck, Lady Constance uttered a delighted shriek, leaped from the step, and flew across the expanse of parquetry floor, both arms outstretched; to cast herself upon the chest of a young gentleman who had that moment entered by the front door, and was handing his hat and gloves to the butler.

'Lady Constance!' said Miss Hartigan, in pained reproof. Her words were not heeded. The Ladies Caroline and Diana, following their sister's example, bounded after her. The new arrival was instantly surrounded. The two younger girls, swinging from each of his arms, began talking both at once. Constance clung to his lapels. Cleeves, the family butler, still waiting to receive his Lordship's coat, regarded the scene with a benign air. Miss Hartigan, tut-tutting after the children, crossed the hall to join the group.

Lord Mainwaring, lifting laughing eyes above Constance's head, saw Bethesda—still standing on the lowest step, alone.

Her hair caught every reflected glint of candlelight and flame. One white arm, with its tapering rosy-tipped fingers, rested lightly on the bannister. A slim foot in white satin was poised, arrested, on the bottom stair. A thick glowing ringlet, coaxed forward by Lady Cumnor's clever maid, lay across the demure bosom of her muslin dress; from its chaste neck frill of white lace her proud young head rose, half-turned, the pure line of chin and cheekbone sharply etched against the dark panelling behind her.

For a long moment their eyes met and held. They stood, all movement suddenly stilled.

Then he gently disengaged the children, and taking Constance's hand in his own, he stepped across the shining floor towards the staircase.

'How do you do, ma'am?' he said. His voice was deep, warm and strong. 'I think you must be Miss Carfax. Connie, love, won't you present me to your friend?'

Bethesda raised her eyes to his like an enchanted princess waking from a spellbound sleep; she was a tall girl, but her head only just topped his shoulder. A coat of many capes swung to his booted heels, and polished Hessians gleamed on his long legs. The heavy drab coat could not disguise the fact that his broad shoulders needed no padding. Nor did he have to worry about a laced corset to draw in his slim waist. His immaculate buckskins were strained across powerful thighs. His eyes, as they looked into her own, were of the deepest, most brilliant blue she had ever seen, and fringed with black lashes that any girl in her right mind would give her soul for. His mouth was enough to set a sculptor instantly groping for his tools of trade; waves of guinea-gold hair gleamed above his white forehead; and black brows, delicately traced, gave just the suggestion of an upward slant away from his beautiful nose. He gave the impression that his skin had been ever so lightly dusted over with gold. His smile revealed strong and perfect teeth, and a single small mole at the corner of his mouth gave character to its classic outline.

In all her life she had never dreamed, or imagined, so splendid a young man. Lips parted, eyes wide, she drowned in that blue gaze, and felt her legs tremble and her knees melt. A warm tide of some hitherto unknown emotion surged deliciously through her veins, broke over her head, and turned her dizzy. The points of light from the candle-sconces dazzled her eyes, and Constance's voice, half-heard, seemed to come from far away. There was a sighing in her ears, and the floor seemed as if it tilted beneath her feet. Somehow, she sank into a creditable curtsey; but ever afterwards she was used to wonder what had saved her from stumbling onto the parquetry before their assembled eyes.

CHAPTER
THREE

THE Michaelmas holidays were past and gone, and winter had come in with a rush. The trees in the grounds of Miss Skeffington's seminary stood bare in the driving wind. Spatters of sleet swept in from the sea. Seated in the parlour with the other boarders, cosily grouped around the fire, their hands busy with the compulsory needlework, Bethesda and Constance could hear cold rain beating on the windows. Branches tapped on the leaded panes. The clipped voice of the English mistress, reading aloud from a book of sermons, went steadily on.

Bethesda heard none of these improving sentences. She was looking back and wondering where she had found the presence of mind, on that final evening at Lady Cumnor's, to conduct herself correctly. She had got herself into the drawing-room with the other girls, and made her polite curtsey to the various guests. She had smiled and replied with pretty deference to the staccato questioning and hard stare of the parrot-beaked Duchess of Andover. Lady Julia, eldest daughter of the house, twenty years old and in proud possession of a rich and doting husband and a hopeful son and heir of six months, had shown a friendly interest, and had engaged her in conversation at some length. She had managed, when requested to do so, to give a respectable performance upon the pianoforte, and had later accompanied while Constance sang some ballads in her sweet soprano voice.

And throughout it all she felt as if she had been thrown over a cliff.

When Marcus, in due course, having changed his riding dress for a black coat of superfine and dovegrey pantaloons, entered the drawing-room to pay his respects to his mother and the company, an intoxicating wave of excitement had set her whole body tingling. But she continued to preserve her composure; restraining the almost intolerable desire to follow him about the room with her eyes, to strain her ears to catch the sound of his voice. When the schoolroom party retired upstairs, after an hour or so, he bowed over her hand and wished her good-night; he gave her one long, intent look; but there had been no chance for any private speech.

And early the next morning, the carriage was there, with Lady Andover enthroned against the cushions, to convey them inexorably back to school.

Now, seated in the quiet parlour, her thoughts continued to run endlessly on, over and over, round the same track, coming always to the same conclusion. Promise or no promise; no matter what happened, she would not, could not under any circumstances marry Maurice Barrington.

Just to think of it made her flesh creep.

If she could not have the Viscount, she would not marry at all. She pictured herself as an old maid, living on sufferance at Ansteys—for a single girl would never be permitted to set up her own establishment—dragging out an unmarried existence, at the beck and call of Amelia and those two horrid little boys. It was a bleak prospect. But she saw no help for it. If Lord Mainwaring did not offer for her—and she had no means of knowing if he had even given her another thought—an old maid she must be.

And of immediate urgency was the matter of her promise, so hastily given, and now so thoroughly regretted, to marry Barrington.

He must release her. He must return her ring. She felt truly sorry at giving him pain, but she had no real doubt that he would free her with a good grace, for he was, in her mind, most truly the gentleman, and would surely understand. She was unhappy at the thought of his disappointment, and felt miserably guilty. The fault was entirely hers. She hoped that he would find it in his heart to forgive her, though to be sure, she did not deserve it.

The pearls that Barrington had given her had been placed in a small neat package in the hollow tree, for the gatekeeper to find and send on. With them was enclosed a short missive, rather desperate in tone. She begged his forgiveness. She was deeply sorry—but she had made a dreadful mistake; she could not marry him after all. She was sure he would understand, and would consider their engagement at an end. Would he please keep strict account of the cost of the gowns and other things, and she would faithfully repay him when she came into her inheritance. She asked urgently that he return her Mama's ring by the earliest post. She would always be grateful to him for his kindness in her need. She signed herself, Yr. Affectionate Friend. And as she sat quietly sewing, she counted anxiously the number of days that must probably elapse before this guileless appeal should reach his London lodgings, and estimated, for the fiftieth time, the length of time before she could hope for his reply.

The teacher's voice droned on; Bethesda stared into the fire. The face of Marcus, constantly in her mind, took shape before her eyes. Just to say his name to herself set her pulses leaping; her body and mind ached for him in a way that was like physical pain. She thought of him while she slept and while she was awake. If this were love, she thought ruefully, then it was not unalloyed happiness, but an awful unceasing longing that could only be eased by the presence of the loved one. She tried to tell herself sternly that to fall in love at first sight was not rational—not possible—could not happen! It made no difference.

She sighed faintly, and Constance, looking anxiously at her friend's shadowed eyes and the wistful droop of her mouth, wondered once more what could be troubling Bethy. She had seemed, since the day of their return to school, not quite well, almost unaware at times of what was said to her. Her affectionate manner towards Constance had not changed, and her abstraction was hidden from casual obervance by the quiet dignity of her composure. Bethesda had learned long since to conceal hurt feelings from the world, and she could not bring herself to inflict upon Constance the story of her own stupid conduct. It was too humiliating; she felt too embarrassed and guilty; she could not speak of it. And then, on top of all else, to admit to Connie that she had crowned her inexcusable folly by falling hopelessly in love with Connie's own brother—!

No, it was not to be thought of; she must forego the release of unloading her troubles on another.

Now, looking at her friend, Constance thought that

she seemed thinner, and her creamy complexion quite transparent. Could it be that, in spite of the pleasure she had derived from the London visit, Bethy was still unhappy at not going home? That could be so. She was deeply attached to Ansteys, and had never, Constance realised sadly, really accepted the cold fact that it was no longer her own home. In fact, though she was wealthy in her own right, Bethesda did not really have a home, nor would have, unless and until she became a married woman. Taking advantage of the mistress's preoccupation with turning a page in the heavy book, Constance leaned forward and patted her friend's hand. Her rather shy blue eyes looked anxiously into Bethesda's face. Bethesda gave a wan smile, and squeezed the little hand warmly in acknowledgement.

The door opened—a welcome interruption to the sermon—and a white-capped maid entered and spoke deferentially to the schoolmistress.

'If you please, ma'am, Miss Skeffington would wish to speak to Miss Carfax, in her study, as soon as is convenient.'

'Miss Carfax, you are excused,' said the English mistress. Bethesda rose, with trembling knees, made her curtsey, and walked sedately to Miss Skeffington's private study. Her hand shook as she tapped on the panelled door. Was it possible that the tell-tale package, with its accompanying letter, had somehow been discovered in its hiding place? If it had—she tried to picture the possible consequences of her folly, and failed. They were too awful to imagine. With wildly beating heart she entered the study and stood quaking before the wide mahogany desk where the lady sat.

She glanced at Miss Skeffington's face, and her fears

began to recede. For the headmistress was smiling be-
nevolently upon her pupil.

'Sit down, my dear,' she said kindly. 'I have received a
letter from Lady Carfax. The contents will surprise
you—but I am sure you will be pleased. I shall be sorry to
lose you, Bethesda, as I have always considered you a
credit to my school; but I know you will continue to live
by the precepts that we have taught you, once you are
out in society.' She picked up an open letter from the
desk, and fitted her eyeglasses to her nose. 'Lady Carfax
informs me that you are to leave this school in one
week's time, in order to join a houseparty at Ansteys. A
private ball is to be held there, and your aunt wishes you
to mingle a little with the ton, before embarking on the
London Session.' Removing her glasses, Miss Skeffington smiled warmly on the girl who sat frozen, struck
dumb with amazement. 'I am happy for your sake, my
dear, and I am sure you are glad to be released, at last,
from the tedium of schooldays. I hope, however, that
you will look back with fondness upon the days you have
spent here with us.'

Bethesda managed, with an effort, to find her
voice.

'Indeed, ma'am, I shall do so,' she answered, rather
huskily. 'I—I have come to regard the seminary as my
second home. You have been very kind to me, and I am
grateful.'

The lady rose, stepped round the desk, and planted a
chaste kiss on her pupil's cheek. 'Thank you, my dear,'
she said, 'and now leave me. I am sure you are looking
forward to acquainting Lady Constance and your other
friends with your exciting news.'

Still feeling dazed, Bethesda managed a creditable

curtsey and got herself out of the room. She hurried upstairs, to the seclusion of her bedroom, for her head was whirling, her heart beating fast. Leaving school! Join a houseparty at Ansteys! A private ball! She sat down on her bed, and pressed her palms to her forehead. Leaving school!

Suddenly she caught her breath as a thought struck her. If she was indeed to make her come-out, then, almost certainly, she would meet Lord Mainwaring again. Her blood suddenly danced through her veins. Eyes sparkling, cheeks aglow, she sprang to her feet and stood before the mirror.

Then with equal abruptness the colour drained from her face. Sir Maurice! He still had her ring in his possession; what if he returned it here, to the school, and it lay in the secret place in the elm, unclaimed—until, perhaps, someone else should find it?

She snatched pen, ink, and writing tablet from her bureau, and scrawled a few hasty words. 'Suddenly leaving school. Please return ring to my nurse, Mrs Addison, at Ansteys. She will give it safely to me. Yr. friend.'

She caught up her cloak and flung it around her. The corridor was empty. She flew downstairs to the side door, slipped outside, and hurried through the grounds to the tree beside the stone bench, where she had sat, so short a time ago, and had—unbelievably—promised to marry a stranger. She reached up and dropped the note into the hiding place. Thank heavens! She sighed with relief. The gatekeeper would sent it on to Sir Maurice. And he had only to forward it to Addy, and all would be well. Her old nurse would ask no questions, and the story of her foolish indiscretion would never be known.

All would be well, in this world which was suddenly the best of all possible worlds.

Just ten days previously, Eustace, Lord Carfax, had strolled unexpectedly into his wife's dressing-room, in the great house in Grosvenor Square. It was the evening hour, and Lord Carfax's portly form was resplendent in full evening dress. Lady Carfax, engrossed fully in the precise positioning of a particularly beautiful diamond aigrette in her pale feathery curls, looked up at her spouse as he entered the rose-coloured and scented boudoir where she sat.

'Why, Carfax!' she exclaimed, in her high, rather breathless voice. 'I thought you was gone out to dine.' A fragile beauty, she took pains to cultivate a restless fluttering manner, in keeping with her ethereal person. A faint look of surprise drew a tiny line between her skilfully darkened brows.

'Wanted a word with you,' replied his Lordship, easing his corseted figure on to a gilded chair. 'Hoped to catch you now.'

The lady nodded, and waved a white delicate hand at her maid, who bobbed and silently withdrew. As the door closed, Amelia said, with a hint of impatience,

'Well, what is it, Eustace? I am very late, and am expected at the Beaulieus'—'

'Young Mainwaring spoke to me today,' answered his Lordship, flicking a lace handkerchief over an immaculate velvet sleeve. 'Sought an interview with me. Saw him this afternoon. In the bookroom. At three o' clock.'

'Oh—yes?' said Amelia, rather absently. Catching sight of herself in the lighted mirror, her attention had strayed. She reached up to touch the diamonds in her hair.

Lord Carfax glanced at her uneasily, cleared his throat, and took the plunge.

'Asked for Bethesda's hand,' he said bluntly.

A hairbrush fell with a clatter on the dressing-table. Lady Carfax turned her head, and stared at her lord, open-mouthed. Her lips moved, but no sound came. Her blue eyes bulged piteously at her husband.

'Now, 'Melie, don't go and fly into one of your states,' Lord Carfax begged. 'I must admit—I was struck all of a heap myself. Dammit! But it seems he met the girl at the Cumnors', two days ago. Asked permission to pay his addresses to her—just as he ought.'

Her ladyship's writhing lips emitted a stifled gasp. Her hands fluttered wildly. Eustace snatched up an embroidered fan from the dressing-table and fanned his stricken spouse.

'She's nearly seventeen, m'dear,' he said, with dogged perseverance. 'Soon we'll have to bring her out. Mainwaring's said nothing to her, of course. Well, he wouldn't; very correct, all that lot; set of crashing bores, if you ask me.'

The lady managed to find her voice.

'Mainwaring!' she uttered, in throbbing tones. 'Mainwaring! That sly chit—that wretch—to have Mainwaring! I'll not bear it—she shall not have him—no, no, no!'

'Now, my girl, just listen to me, if you please,' said his lordship, with unusual firmness. 'Just stop, for a minute, and think. It's an ideal match for the girl. It would save us a great deal of trouble. Married from the schoolroom; to London's biggest catch. That would give the gossips something to smart about. I mean—nobody could say, could they, that you hadn't done your duty by her.'

The nervous hands wavered and grew still. That was true. Certain censorious ladies, whose criticism of her careless guardianship had irritated her, would have to stop their carping tongues. So brilliant a marriage for the girl would reflect gratifying credit on her aunt.

'And then, you'd be saved all the trouble of her come-out, and steering her through the season,' her husband pointed out. 'As the Viscountess Mainwaring, she would be presented at the Drawing-Room—Lady Cumnor would see to all that. We'd save a deal of expense for a coming-out ball, gowns and so on. And as soon as she's married, she's off our hands, for good and all.'

Lady Carfax sat struggling with conflicting emotions. Her soul rose in revolt against the notion of that school-room miss whom she loathed and always would snaring Cumnor's heir in the matrimonial net. Every girl in London would tear her hair in envy and despair. The chit would be feted, admired, her social position and her future assured. Countess of Cumnor! The wretch! Just to think of it made the lady feel sick; she curled her fingers into talons.

And yet—and yet—the prudent good sense of her husband's words could not help but appeal to her native shrewdness. What he said was true enough. It would be a relief to be rid of the girl for once and for all. And no-one, not even Amelia's most devoted critics, would ever be able to accuse her of not doing anything for her niece. As she was not, herself, an intimate of the Countess's, her future contact with Bethesda would probably be limited to polite acknowledgment across the room at Almack's, or formal nods at such gatherings where they would meet casually as fellow guests. The prospect was most pleasing.

Finally, the saving of expense carried considerable weight. Lady Carfax was forever running into debt, and the cost of launching a debutante upon the town was high. In this way, married from the schoolroom, the enormous expenditure and trouble involved in a first season would be avoided. Only the wedding would have to be paid for. And even that would have to come out of Carfax's pocket, for there was no way in which either Eustace or herself could dip their fingers into Bethesda's fortune. They had settled that point, long ago, with their lawyer Turvey. The knowledge had caused Amelia many bitter reflections. Even if Bethesda died unmarried, the money would revert in its entirety back to her mother's family. The girl's father had made quite certain that his spendthrift brother and featherbrained wife would never see a penny of it. Thinking of this again, Amelia suffered a painful spasm. Thinking of all that money flowing into the already brimming coffers of the Cumnor family made her feel even worse.

But . . .

She turned her rather prominent china-blue eyes to her lord, in unaccustomed appeal.

'What shall I do, Eustace?' she said at last, in quavering tones.

His lordship gave a sigh of relief.

'No need to make a fuss, m'dear,' he said, reassuringly. 'Just take this chance that's offered, and be thankful you are saved a deal of trouble. Get her home from that school; buy her some toggery; ask Mainwaring to the houseparty at Ansteys. Let him pop the question. See if Bethesda will have him.'

'If she will have him!' the lady gasped. 'My lord, have you lost your wits? No girl in her right mind would refuse him!'

'Yes, yes, I feel sure you are right,' said his lordship comfortably, and rose to take his leave. 'I bid you good-night, my love; I have been stayed for this half-hour. But I am glad that your good sense has prevailed in this matter.'

CHAPTER
FOUR

BETHESDA, snuggled on lace pillows in her own dear bedroom at Ansteys, watched dreamily as her maid Betty replenished the fire for the night. Outside, the rich velvet lawns, the forested park, the two ornamental lakes from which arose sweeping terraces which in summer were massed in climbing roses and honeysuckle, all lay wrapped in the stillness of a country night. The huge Tudor house, built on the ruins of a medieval castle and added to by successive generations of Carfaxes, had settled to rest. No sound penetrated the thick walls of Bethesda's room, and if it had, she would not have heard it. For late to-night, Marcus would arrive at Ansteys. He would sleep under its roof. When she rose in the morning, he would be there. Snug in her warm bed, awaiting the morrow, she lay in delicious comfort, while her mind ranged incredulously over the events of the days just past. The journey from school to London—the visit to Amelia's very own, very expensive dressmaker—the gowns for walking, riding, evening parties; gloves, bonnets, shawls, tippets, sandals, boots; gew-gaws and furbelows of all kinds that had been showered upon her dazed person—it all still seemed totally unbelievable. Amelia, with a pretty smile upon her lips and seething anger in her heart, had made quite a touching ceremony of bestowing upon Bethesda her Mama's jewel-casket, and all its contents. And on arrival at Ansteys, the reason for Amelia's amazing and unprecedented generosity and amiability had been revealed. Lord Carfax had acquainted Bethesda with the rapturous news that Lord Mainwaring had asked permission to pay his addresses; that he was bidden to join the houseparty; and that he was expected that very night; after travelling south from the family estates in Yorkshire.

The problem of what to do with the things she had received from Barrington had caused her some anxiety. In the end, they had been bestowed upon an ecstatic housemaid at the school, a lass of Bethesda's own age, who would never in the ordinary way hope to possess garments of such quality. Bethesda had explained to Dolly that as she had no money for a parting gift, perhaps this would do instead? It had solved the problem happily all round, for Dolly had been her particular maid at the seminary, and was entitled to a vail when her mistress should leave; and Bethesda felt no qualms at thus giving away Barrington's largesse, since she had pleged her word to pay him the full cost of the clothes when her money was paid into her hands; she did not think he would have any objection to her making Dolly a parting gift of them. So the little matter was satisfactorily settled to the pleasure of both parties, and Bethesda then thought no more about it.

However, as she moved her body luxuriously under the well-warmed linen sheets, curled in her own four-poster with its blue velvet hangings, half-aware of the noiseless progress of Betty as she moved to and fro on the thick bedroom carpet, she suffered a return of the faint uneasy chill that crept through her veins, now and then, whenever she remembered that Sir Maurice had not yet returned her ring. Common sense told her that there had not yet been time for him to do so. But she felt a tiny thread of anxiety, which kept returning, and would do so until the little carved gold circlet rested safely on her finger once more. She assured herself that there was nothing to worry about. Sir Maurice was so gentlemanly, so understanding. Her termination of the engagement was sure to have caused him pain; she felt sorry for it. But she was sure he would forgive her, and understand. He might have only just received her letter. She would soon hear from him; it would serve no cause to worry; and in the meantime—to-morrow—she would see Marcus again. Hugging the thought to her, she settled herself to sleep, smiling, her face turned into the pillow.

A short, whispered conversation at the bedroom door, and the soft-footed approach of her maid towards the bed where she lay, scarcely penetrated her consciousness. It was not until the velvet curtains were drawn back, and she opened her eyes to see Betty's face above her, faintly frowning, that her senses became alert. She saw, with a sudden thump of her heart, that the maid held a letter in her hand.

'Miss Bethesda—are you awake?' Betty whispered. 'I'm sure I don't know if I ought to give this to you—but it was handed to one of the under-gardeners at the lodge gate; and he brought it to the scullery door; and he was to tell you, Miss, that the gentleman as gave it said you would be very pleased to receive it.'

Bethesda reached out for the letter. Her hand trembled visibly, and the puzzled frown deepened on Betty's anxious face.

'It's quite all right, Betty, really it is,' Bethesda said

faintly. 'Give me the letter and leave the candles. And—and Betty, you won't speak of this to my aunt?'

The maid had grown elderly in Carfax service. She had been in the household when that long-mourned elder brother had died, and at Bethesda's birth. She loved the girl dearly, and still considered Amelia an usurper of what was rightly their young lady's. She also knew that if a whisper of this should come to Lady Carfax's ears, she—Betty—would instantly be dismissed, turned out of doors without a character; and at her age, it would be very hard to find another place. But the water-green eyes were looking so pleadingly into her own, and, after some hesitation, she said,

'All right, Miss Bethy, I won't tell, and nor will the others. But—you are not in any trouble, are you? I couldn't face your Mama again, not on the Judgment Day, if it were so, and I kept silent.'

'No, no, it's all right, truly,' said Bethesda desperately. 'Just leave me now, please, dear Betty, I'll snuff the candles myself. I shan't need you again to-night. Go to bed.'

'Very well,' said Betty, and withdrew. As the heavy door closed behind her, Bethesda ripped open the letter with shaking fingers.

It was very short. There was no signature.

'Certainly you shall have your ring. But I should like to bid you farewell in person. Come to the fountain garden below the last terrace as soon as you can. I am waiting there.'

Bethesda gave a gasp of wild relief and exultation. She leaped from her bed and threw the note on the fire. She flew across the vast rich carpet to her massive wardrobe. Hurriedly she scrambled into a woollen gown and a

cloak whose hood hid her bright hair. Opening the
bedroom door, she peered out cautiously, and saw that
the long corridor was deserted. Familiar with every inch
of the rambling mansion, she then proceeded to make
her way, by various passages, half-flights, and diverse
turns, to the ground floor. Here she entered the garden-
room which was used by the housekeeper to arrange the
great vases of flowers that adorned the house. The
garden-room opened directly into a walled flower-
garden, where there was a stout outer door to be unbolted. But the bolts, after a short struggle, slid back
with only a faint squeak. If Betty should return to her
bedroom, Bethesda prayed that she would think her
mistress asleep. She had snuffed the candles and left the
room in darkness. It was a chance that had to be taken.

She went cautiously across the first terrace, her feet
crunching on the frosted grass. From here, successive
flights of shallow stone steps, flanked by tall urns which
in summer overflowed with scented blossoms, led down
and down to a secluded court. Here, in the warm
months, a fountain played, beside the smaller of the
artificial lakes. This fountain garden was surrounded on
three sides by its own luxuriant shrubbery; the fourth
side gave access to a stout tall garden gate, which opened
into a side lane lined with hedgerows; this in turn wound
its way in due course to the road.

It was a secret, shadowy place, well-suited to a clan-
destine meeting. But she felt no uneasiness; every foot
of the grounds was well known to her; she could have
found the place blindfold. She did wonder briefly at his
skill in arranging illicit meetings at night. It was almost
like a re-enactment of the episode at the Seminary. She
quickly suppressed the thought. He had said that she

should have her ring back; and, in the light of the way she had treated him, the wish to bid farewell to her in person was not at all unreasonable. She would stay but a few minutes, and would be safely back indoors long before she was missed.

With thankfulness in her heart, and words of gratitude and apology on her lips, she moved into the dark stillness of the fountain court.

The words were never uttered.

A black shadow moved behind her. But before she could turn, a heavy scarf was whipped around her face from behind, and pulled tight. The next moment, a cloth was flung over her head, falling to her knees; and fighting and struggling, choking for air, her voice muffled, she felt herself lifted and carried by what seemed to be more than one set of powerful arms. She kicked furiously. One foot found its mark, and she heard a faint curse. But her head began to swim, and she hardly realised when she was thrown roughly up into a carriage that waited with dimmed lamps in the quiet lane beyond the gate. The door slammed shut, the horses were whipped up, and the coach moved off swaying, to where the road stretched away across the dark empty country-side. With a lurch that sent her reeling back against the squabs, they took the corner into the road; and the horses bounded forward under the lash.

The cloth was pulled from her head and tossed aside. She stared into the face of Maurce Barrington.

Her first reaction was one of blind fury. Ten generations of feudal privilege rose in outrage at this insulting treatment. Before he could draw back, she raked at him with her nails like a tigress, lashing out at that smiling face. Then she launched herself at the carriage door, clawing at the handle, screaming through the twisted gag. The handle resisted her efforts, but she managed to get one arm through the window, grabbing futilely at the outside air, before Barrington caught her and hauled her back, kicking and clawing, and threw her flat on the carriage seat with a thud that knocked her breathless.

'You vixen,' he panted, gripping her arms, and crushing her body with the weight of his own, as she twisted and writhed on the seat. Her strong small teeth met in the cloth that was partly stifling her cries. Her head suddenly rocked sideways as he hit her with a stinging slap across the face. He took her shoulders and shook her viciously.

'Be still, or by God, I'll throttle you!' he rasped. His fingers dug into her soft throat. 'Stop it, unless you want to be choked unconscious!' The ugly note in his voice warned her that he was in earnest. The blood began to roar in her ears. If she were unconscious she could not possibly escape from him; and every minute was taking her farther away from Ansteys.

She closed her eyes and let her body go limp. Slowly, the crushing fingers relaxed and drew away from her neck. She felt him fumbling at the gag.

Neither of them had perceived, during their brief struggle, the laden travelling-coach that had passed them in the opposite direction; moving at speed along the quiet road behind a team of sweet-stepping bays, towards the main gate of Ansteys.

'Now!' said Barrington, breathing fast—for her supple body twisting against his own had stirred his senses, to a degree that even surprised himself—'Now, madam, let me explain certain things to you—things that you seem to have forgotten.' By God, she was a spitfire and no mistake. Well, it would give him much pleasure to tame her. It would add a spice to matrimony. She would pay—he promised silently—and pay handsomely for the scratch her nails had dealt him. He could feel a warm trickle of blood on his face. She would beg his pardon for that, humbly and contritely; the thought gave him a pleasing thrill. 'You seem to have forgotten, my lady, that we are betrothed. Word has reached my ears that you are to be married. That is true; you are to be married to me. I mean to hold you to your promise.'

She flung herself back against the cushions, as far away from him as possible. Her chin lifted. Her eyes blazed at him.

'You lie!' she spat at him. 'I am not betrothed to you! I will not marry you!'

He laughed mockingly.

'But I wear your ring, my love,' he pointed out. 'Your pledge of undying affection. I am certain that there are any number of persons who would recognise it. I have it here—on my finger.' He studied her for a moment, and then patted the breast pocket of his coat. 'I have also a letter written by you, in which you accept my proposal of marriage, and make reference to certain items I purchased for you. At considerable expense, I might add—still, you will reimburse me for that, many times over—and as well as that, you took from me a string of pearls—as you so obligingly specified in your letter. A splendid letter, ma'am—my felicitations! If I had dictated it myself, I could not have bettered it.'

There was a long silence. She gazed at him in horror as gradually the implications of his words sank into her brain. Slowly, inexorably, the anger that had upheld her began to ebb away. As the full realisation of the trap into which she had fallen struck home, she was assailed by a sick cold fear. Bravely, she tried to hide the sudden trembling of her body, as she held herself upright, and spoke through shaking lips.

'You also received from me two other letters. In the first of these, I clearly terminated our engagement. I returned the pearls to you.'

'Your second and third missives have been destroyed,' he answered, his thin mouth curling in a sneer. 'They have never existed—as far as I am concerned. And the pearls I have here—in my pocket. Presently, I can assure you, you will be glad to allow me to fasten them about your neck.' As he spoke he reached out a hand to touch her throat; his gaze slid down to the firm swell of her breast; his face, its thin mouth smiling in that hateful sneer, bent closer towards her own. She felt his breath on her cheek as he said, 'Why not make the best of it, my lady? There is no way out for you. I have evidence in my possession that will blacken your name forever. Come, let us be friends; I shall ask nothing of you as a wife, except that you do not interfere with my pursuits, and that your taste in dress should do me credit. Is it a bargain?'

A violent shudder shook her from head to foot. She strained away from him, and spoke almost against his lips, in a vehement whisper.

'If you dare even to *touch* me,' she hissed, 'I shall be sick!'

'Very well, have it your own way,' he gritted. 'But you will beg my forgiveness for that remark.' He looked fixedly into her face for a few moments; but then, to her relief, he drew away and leaned back, staring moodily in front of him.

With her flesh creeping at the very thought of his mouth on her own, Bethesda sat silent. A wave of black despair threatened to overwhelm her. Only pride stopped her from bursting into wild sobs, begging him to pity her, to take her home before her absence was discovered. The thought that Marcus might even now actually be arriving at Ansteys turned her almost frantic. How thoroughly deluded she had been! How blind, how unbelievably stupid! She almost launched a desperate appeal for mercy; but instinct told her it was no use. An appeal to his compassion would fall on deaf ears, for he was, she realised, quite devoid of any such. She had been totally deceived in him. Upheld only by her determination not to break down, she sat on in dumb misery; as the horses galloped through the night.

The carriage left the main road and began jolting along a dark winding lane, little better than a cart track. The wheels skidded, the coach slewed around on deep ruts and loose stones. Once or twice it seemed that they must overturn, or end in the ditch. But at length, after half an hour of bone-shaking lurching and jolting, they drew rein before a small squat building, apparently a cottage. The carriage halted; the door was flung open; and Bethesda, arms twisted behind her back, was jostled along a short uneven path, through a narrow door and into a mean little parlour, low-beamed and sparsely furnished. It was lit only by a hanging lamp, whose beams could not penetrate the thick curtain with which the solitary window was covered.

'The cottage is empty,' grinned Barrington, 'and very isolated. Don't bother to scream, ma'am, nobody will hear. Hobden is on guard outside—and so we shall not be disturbed, my dear, until such time as I choose to take you back to Ansteys. We shall go back together, and you will present me to your guardians as your affianced husband.'

'Never!' she said huskily. 'Never! I won't do it! I shall die first!'

He looked at her, as she stood facing him, tall and splendid, her proud head thrown back. Her hair caught copper lights from the smokey lamp, and her hands were gripped together to stop their shaking. He watched her, his eyes glinting, and his voice thickened as he answered.

'But you won't die, ma'am. You will be glad to marry me, or indeed, to marry anyone who is not too fastidious to take my leavings. Oh, yes; you will beg me, on your knees, to marry you . . . I promise you that!'

Breathing fast, he lunged forward, and caught her arm; he swung her roughly round, and twisted his hand in the bodice of her gown, to rip it away from her shoulders. She brought her heel down on his instep, and wrenched herself away. She sprang back against the wall, her eyes burning green fire in her white face.

'If you come near me—be sure I will kill you!' she choked, and he saw the dangerous gleam of her narrowed eyes, and the curl of her fingers into talons.

He laughed aloud. It was going to be even more enjoyable than he had thought. Subduing a tigress was what stirred a man's blood most of all. Much more stimulating than ravishing a weeping shivering schoolgirl —which was what he had expected. The best part of any amorous adventure, he reflected with satisfaction, was in reducing a rebellious female to submission. A horse, or a woman, it was the same; the true excitement, the deepest intoxication, came from breaking their spirit.

Once the fight went out of them, and they became
docile, the dish lost its savour.

Neither of them was aware of the noiseless opening of
the door at the far end of the room.

'A taste of the lash is what you need, my dear,'
Barrington said, and laughed again, on a high-pitched
note.

A clipped voice, vibrating with cold and deadly fury,
spoke suddenly from the shadows, beyond the circle of
lamplight.

'I think not, Barrington,' it said, with ominous quiet.

In the open doorway, his shoulders almost blocking
the narrow aperture, his eyes gleaming like blue quartz
in the reflected light, stood the Viscount Mainwaring.

Barrington swore furiously, and swung about to face
the intruder. Bethesda, dizzy and half-fainting, stunned
with the suddenness of it, leaned against the wall, her
hands spread out on either side. Numb with shock, she
stared, lips parted, as his lordship kicked the door shut
and advanced to where Barrington stood.

The Viscount's eyes glittered with lethal fire. His
black brows met across his nose. His mouth was set in a
granite line; and two white dents marked the edges of his
nostrils.

'Miss Carfax,' he said with formal courtesy between
clenched teeth, 'my coach is waiting at the gate. Be so
good as to go to it and get inside. My regrets that I cannot
escort you, but I have business here. It will not take
long.'

Unable to think or question, she moved away from the
wall, in blind response to his voice. But before she had
taken a step, Barrington sprang forward to bar her way.

'Wait!' he cried hoarsely. 'Wait, Mainwaring, if you

please! You do not know the truth! Hear it! Hear what the deceitful jade has done; she has promised herself to me—she has accepted gifts from me she has met me in secret, while she was still at school! Fine conduct! See— she gave me her own mother's ring; I wear it here, on my finger. Read the letter she wrote to me, of her own free will; read it—and judge for yourself! She is a wanton!'

He fumbled in his coat and withdrew the letter. With shaking hand he proffered it to Lord Mainwaring. Marcus twitched the paper from his hand, tossed it on the floor; and proceeded to shrug himself out of his driving coat. Barrington, reading the purpose in the Viscount's eyes, retreated until the wall stopped his backward progress; and then, in the face of his lordship's ominous advance, of necessity put up his fists.

They were both tall men, and Barrington, with the furious rage of a cornered rat, rushed suddenly forward, hurling himself on his opponent, trying to bear him down. But he was no match for the Viscount, whose taut young body was as strong as steel and supple as a young sapling. There was a swaying to and fro, a short flurry of blows; the lamp swung wildly and shadows danced on the rough walls. Then the Viscount connected with a fine flush hit to the jaw that lifted the other off his feet and slammed him against the wall. Barrington sagged, slid gently to the floor, and lay still.

'I ought to have killed him,' said his lordship with regret. He stirred the recumbent form with his boot. 'But it would make a damned scandal, and we can't risk it.' He leaned and lifted one of Barrington's flaccid hands, removed from it a small gold ring, and proffered this to Bethesda. 'Is this your ring? Here—my poor child, let me put it on your hand. And then I must get you safe home, before they find you missing and start a hue and cry.'

He stepped towards her, took her hand, and slipped the ring on her finger. At the touch of his hand on her own, her cheeks flamed suddenly with warm colour. She lifted her eyes to his; they gazed at each other for a long moment. Then she was crushed in his arms.

Their mouths met and clung. Locked in his embrace, hard against his great chest, she seemed to be spinning and turning like the turning lamp. Her flesh dissolved and melted into his, as she was swept by a rush of wild and passionate feeling such as she had never dreamed of. Half fainting, she soared away into a new dimension of being; and in that moment, gave herself to him forever.

'You're mine, you know,' the Viscount said at last, smoothing the rippling hair that rioted upon his shoulder. 'I love you; I knew it at the first moment. I had meant to ask you to-morrow, but under the circumstances . . . Will you marry me, love?'

Tears rose to her eyes. She freed herself from his arms, and turned away, burying her face in her hands. Then she burst into weeping.

'But I can't—you must know I can't,' she cried. 'I have been so wicked, so stupid. All that he said is true. Read the letter—see for yourself! You—you could never marry such a one!'

His lordship picked up the letter. Holding it by one corner, he brought it close to the lamp's oily flame. The letter caught—little flames crept across the white paper. He dropped the smouldering remnants on the floor and ground them under his heel. His cerulean eyes glinted at her; a slow smile crept over his mouth.

'Miss Carfax,' he said sternly, 'I feel I must point out

to you that having kissed any gentleman as you have just kissed me, you must instantly accompany him to the altar! You can do no less! Now—' he placed a hand beneath her chin, and turned her face towards him. 'Must I kneel down upon this damned dirty floor, madam? If you insist upon it, then I'll do it; but if you could find it in your heart to spare me—'

To her own amazement she felt a bubble of laughter rising through her tears. Her heart gave such a leap of joyousness that she could scarcely breathe. She drew herself up, and white hands gracefully poised, she swept him a deep obeisance.

'Sir,' she whispered, and the dimple showed beside her mouth, 'you do me too much honour.'

'My darling!' responded the Viscount. He caught her hands and drew her to her feet. 'Now quickly, love. We must leave this place.' Together they hurried from the cottage and down the rough path. Near the gate stood his Lordship's man, pistol levelled at the head of Barrington's servant. Marcus flung a fold of his coat over Bethesda's face and paused to speak to the man as they went past him.

'Your master's inside. He ain't dead—more's the pity. If I hear a whisper of this night's work, be sure I shall know where lies the blame; and be equally sure that I shall settle the account in full. Both of you get away from here; and don't let me clap eyes on you again. Do you understand me?'

A low mutter of acquiescence came from the dark figure.

The Viscount handed his lady up into his carriage, and the door closed upon them.

Leaning against his shoulder, her hand in his as they

jolted and swayed back along the track, she said, timidly.

'My lord, how did you know—how did you find me?'

'I saw an arm thrust from a carriage window and heard a faint cry,' he replied. 'I recognised Barrington's turn-out; those yellow wheels are enough to turn a man queasy. I guessed he was up to some mischief; Martin turned the horses and we followed. When he took this side-track I was sure he was up to no good. We had to take some care on this rough surface—else I should have come upon you sooner. I am sorry that you had to endure the company of that stinking rat even for a moment. It won't happen again.'

'When I saw you—' she said, very low, 'I—I could not believe it. I had lost my courage, and was so afraid.'

The arm around her waist tightened into an embrace that crushed her ribs. The Viscount's free hand flexed into a serviceable fist.

'I wish I had killed him,' he growled. 'But don't worry; he won't trouble you again. How came you, my love, to get yourself into such a pickle? Barrington's well known around the town. He's a gambler, y'know—pockets to let; he dropped ten thousand in a single night at Brooks. He has been chasing after every heiress in the country for years. How did he contrive to meet you?'

'Oh—Marcus!' she wailed. She turned her face into his shoulder. Between tears and sobs, as they jolted through the darkness, the whole sorry little story came tumbling out.

The Viscount smoothed her hot forehead and dried her cheeks with his own handkerchief. A cold anger burned in him as the sad little tale was told. The trap had been set by a master hand, and she had walked so blindly into it. If he had not happened to recognise Barrington's carriage—! His impulse was to turn back immediately and dispatch Sir Maurice to perdition. But, little as he liked it, the most important thing was that Bethesda be returned to the protection of her own roof without a moment's delay. Furthermore, if this story ever became known, her name would be on every tongue; bandied about the clubs; nothing would restore her lost reputation.

Considering the matter carefully, as they plunged on through the darkness, he decided that it was unlikely that Barrington would open his mouth. Without Bethesda's letter and ring he had not a shred of proof concerning the matter. Safe in the protection of his own family launched into society under the wing of his mother the Countess and his aunt Andover, he could not forsee any way in which Barrington could harm Bethesda. If he did attempt to start any malicious gossip, he would be ridiculed—he had been trying to fix his interest with an heiress, or any woman endowed with a fortune, for years; it had become a standing joke. If he was mad enough to try and start tongues wagging, no-one would believe him. And—also—he would know that the Viscount's vengeance would be swift and immediate. No— Sir Maurice could wait. Silently, the Viscount promised himself the pleasure of one of these days settling the score more fully than had been possible to-night.

When the coach drew up at the garden gate by which Bethesda had been abducted from the grounds, it went much against his lordship's will to let her go, alone, up across the darkened terraces, the way she had come. But there was no help for it. One final embrace and clasp of hands, and she slipped through the gate. He could only hope that the bustle of his own arrival at the great iron gates, where a low light burned in the lodge, would mask any sound that she might make as she regained the sanctuary of the house.

CHAPTER
FIVE

THE tenth Baron Carfax regarded the young couple before him with an indulgent eye.

'Well, well,' he said. 'You are two very fortunate young people, to be sure!'

They made, he thought, a remarkably handsome pair. The girl would certainly make a sensation in town. And it was a love match; no doubt about that. He was pleased for Bethesda's sake. Though he had never in the past bestirred himself on her behalf, he had sometimes thought that his beautiful wife could have given a little more attention to his brother's only surviving child. However, all had turned out for the best. It was a remarkable stroke of fortune that Mainwaring should tumble into love with the girl. He had been hunted from pillar to post by every match-making mama in town. Now Bethesda would be off their hands, brilliantly established and with relatively little expense. Capital!

Lady Carfax came fluttering into the salon where the young pair sat on a curved satin sofa, facing the fire-place, before which stood Eustace, a heavy arm along the carved mantelpiece. Amelia was a vision in delicate primrose gauze, her blonde hair styled in the Medusa, her face delicately tinted by the skilled hand of her maid. With her rosy mouth prettily pouting, she came lightly tripping across the room and addressed the Viscount in sugary tones.

'My lord, such a charming letter from your sweet Mama,' she said. 'I shall pen a reply as soon as may be. Dearest Lady Cumnor! She wishes to have Bethesda back again, for a visit. But I have a better plan; as soon as the ball is over, to-morrow night, let us all remove to Grosvenor Square. For your mother and I, Marcus, will have so much to discuss. The wedding—the guests—the bridal clothes. There is so much to be done!'

A fleeting vision of this restless little hummingbird and his stately mother enjoying a comfortable discussion, their heads together over the teacups, crossed the Viscount's mind and caused him to suppress a grin.

'That sounds like a excellent plan, ma'am,' he answered. 'For with your permission, Bethesda and I have fixed upon an Easter wedding. When we are married, my mother will hold a dress-ball, to present her into society as my wife; and she will make her entree into court circles under the aegis of my aunt Andover.'

A fierce qualm pierced the lady's heart, for it was too bad to have to pretend, and to congratulate the wretched girl before whom stretched such a glittering future, and all handed to her on a platter, without the least push or effort! Just because she was born with looks—though for her part, Amelia had always considered that particular combination of red hair and green eyes excessively vulgar.

Great overgrown thing, Amelia thought spitefully. No-one will ever call her Titania, or sprite, or compare her with a drift of thistledown. Tossing her head so that her pale curls danced, she smiled brilliantly upon the Viscount, and said,

'Why—my lord—that is very soon! I am not sure that it can be so quickly arranged—'

'I wish it, and so does Bethesda,' said the Viscount firmly. 'And she shall do just as she wishes, now and always.' His blue eyes rested thoughtfully upon her ladyship. 'And I might add, ma'am, that in addition to studying her wishes, I mean to take care of her as well. I promise you that.'

There was a silence. Amelia, taken aback, began to utter some hasty words, while her cheeks mantled with angry colour.

'What can you mean?' she demanded shrilly. 'Do you dare to imply—'

She stopped. The Viscount's brows were drawn together across his nose. Before the steady regard of his eyes, she faltered, and caught herself up.

'Well . . . well, that is very proper of you, I am sure,' she said at last. 'An Easter wedding—there can be no real objection, I suppose. I shall discuss it with the Countess, when we meet. Carfax, have you anything to say?'

'Nothing, my dear,' answered her spouse, who was enjoying a guilty pleasure at the sight of Amelia worsted in a battle of wills, however briefly. It would be, his lordship reflected, a novel experience for her.

'Then that is settled,' Amelia pouted. She turned to the door. 'I shall immediately write to your mother, Marcus. How I long to see her!'

She departed. Eustace, leaning upon the mantel, noticed that Bethesda was looking rather pale and heavy-eyed. He supposed her to be overset by the excitement of her lover's arrival. Certainly, Mainwaring had reached Ansteys very late; much later than the sleepy butler and housekeeper, waiting for the sound of carriage wheels on the long driveway, could have wished for.

'You look a bit washed out, m'dear,' he remarked. 'And Mainwaring, you must be weary too. What time did you arrive?'

'Just on two o'clock, sir,' Marcus answered promptly. 'I had hoped to be here sooner, but my right wheeler went a trifle lame, and we had to come by easy stages; there are no posting-inns, as you know, once past the Eltham turn-off.'

'Yes,' Eustace agreed, stirring the fire with his foot. 'Very lonely country hereabouts; good for the hunt, though. Well, sooner you than me, m'boy. I slept like a log myself—always do. So did 'Melie—well, she has to! Doses herself, you know, with those fool laudanum drops. Says the silence of the country keeps her awake. Don't see it myself,' continued his lordship, warming to his subject. 'How can silence keep a person awake? But you can't argue with a female. Remember that, my boy.' Pondering the thought, he stared into the fire. Bethesda and Marcus exchanged a fleeting smile. Rousing himself, Lord Carfax said,

'Now, you can't sit there all day, y'know, billin' and cooin'. Care to go riding? I can offer you a nice-ish hack, Mainwaring, well up to your weight. And there's my lady's mare for you, Beth; she hasn't had it out for days and it needs exercising. Besides, she rides like a heap of stones, for all she's so small. Not like you girl—you've got your father's seat on a horse. Now then—over the downs for a gallop. What do you say?'

The plan was agreed to with pleasure, and Bethesda promised not to keep the gentlemen waiting for long.

She sped upstairs and summoned Betty to help her into her new riding habit. The severe garment, made of fine black cloth, fitted her closely, and was worn with a black velvet hat turned up on one side, a white cravat of lace and muslin, and serviceable leather gloves. The classic plainness of this ensemble set off admirably her startling colouring and the chiselled lines of her face. A bruise from Barrington's grasping fingers marked one side of her throat, above the collar-bone. It was hidden by her cravat. She hoped it would fade by the following evening, when she would be wearing her new white evening gown at Amelia's ball. However, if it did not, there was a solution at hand. Among the contents of her mother's jewel-casket, so recently bestowed upon her by Amelia, there rested a particularly beautiful pearl-and-emerald collar, which though fine and delicate, would be sufficiently wide to hide the tell-tale mark.

She hurried down the staircase, the fish-tailed skirt of her riding dress caught up over her arm, revealing spurred black boots on her long legs. The gentlemen were waiting for her on the wide shallow semi-circle of steps that led up to the front door. Eustace gave an approving nod at sight of her. Marcus felt a surge of love and pride. The grooms were ready with the horses. Bolton tossed Bethesda into the saddle. She settled lightly upon Firefly's back, and Marcus saw at once the significance of Lord Carfax's remark. With the possible exception of his sister Constance, he had never seen a lady with a better seat on horseback. He had not thought that she might be an accomplished rider; and would not have cared if she had not. But he looked forward with sudden keen pleasure to providing her with a mount that would do her justice, when they were married. In his stables in Yorkshire was a certain black gelding, recently acquired; beautifully mouthed, spirited, a sweet stepper. Noting the gentle precision of Bethesda's hands, he promised himself the pleasure of presenting her with Nightbird for her very own hack.

'And I'll teach you to drive, too,' he said, following his thought aloud, as they waited for the main gates to be thrown back. The mare was restive after several days in her stall, and suddenly took high-bred exception to the scurrying leaf on the gravel. Her sudden sideways leap did not discompose her rider; with sure hands and caressing voice she gentled the nervous creature, and from under the brim of her saucy hat she threw the Viscount a sparkling glance.

'My lord, I can handle the ribbons,' she assured him. 'Papa taught me, almost before I walked! I was used to mount his hunters almost from babyhood. In recent years, I have not had a great deal of practice; but I have retained the skill, I believe.'

'I am sure of it,' he answered, and as always when their eyes met, a spark seemed to leap between them, and they travelled together, for a moment, to another time and place. Behind them, Lord Carfax spoke in plaintive tones.

'The gates are open,' he pointed out.

Through the great park they went, and along a well-marked bridle path; then up across the common to a vantage point from which, before them, rolled the open country. The grasses shivered in the keen wind that blew in from the cold grey sea. 'To the farthest tree!' Bethesda cried, and the mare, just touched by the spur, bounded off. Marcus gathered up the big-boned bay and took after her. They raced across the thick grass, sharp airs whipping their faces, bringing the blood to their cheeks. Little by little the big horse overhauled the gallant little mare.

But—'By Gad,' thought Lord Carfax, following the flying figures with his eyes as he cantered comfortably along in their wake—'If they were equally mounted, she would certainly outrun him.'

'Oh, Miss Bethesda,' the maid Betty breathed, regarding her mistress with eyes clouded and misty. 'How beautiful you are, lovey! If your dear mother could only see you this minute!'

Bethesda stood before the long mirror in her brightly-lit bedroom and looked at herself. The great house was ablaze from end to end with light. All afternoon at intervals assorted carriages had arrived, disgorging those guests who had been bidden to the ball at Ansteys and would have to be accommodated overnight, on account of the distance. Presently, they would all sit down to dine, a company of twenty. When the dancing began at ten o'clock, in the great room built for the purpose at the back of the house, the numbers would be swelled to four times as many, as the local county members arrived to dance the night away. An air of bustle and suppressed excitement had affected the whole household during the intervening hours; for it was by now an open secret, from the family butler down to the newest and humblest scullery-maid, that their young lady was betrothed; and that the announcement was to be formally made, on this very evening, to the assembled guests at her ladyship's private ball. The happy news had spread like wildfire, throughout the estate, the village, the entire country, it seemed; and much was the exclaiming, the astonishment, the rejoicing—especially on the part of the older generation who had known Bethesda's parents, and remembered their marriage. But all the servants, old and new, were caught up in the general air of festivity; and Mrs Wirth, the impeccable housekeeper and benevolent despot of the household, had been obliged to reprove Jenny, the newest and flightiest of the kitchenmaids, when she came upon that damsel describing to a rapt audience how his lordship had smiled straight at her on the stairs, and almost caused her to swoon dead away.

The gown of white satin fell in shimmering silvery folds to her feet. Her shining hair was caught into a knot on the crown of her head, and thence allowed to fall in gleaming thick ringlets to her shoulders. A pearl comb was set behind the curls on the back of her head, and the pearl-and-emerald collar was clasped around the smooth column of her throat. She wore gloves of white French kid, and the bracelets that matched the necklace were fastened around her wrists, over the gloves. A white pearl-embroidered fan completed the ensemble. Since she was not yet officially out, the neckline of her gown was modestly cut, but it was low enough to reveal the delicious curve of her white bosom, which was no less white than the softly-glistening sheath of satin which clung to her figure and followed the long graceful line of torso before dissolving into fullness. Betty, watching her mistress, wiped her eyes, and reflected that although the pearl-and-emerald set might be thought too opulent for a young lady of sixteen to wear, Miss Bethesda was so magnificent that she could carry it off; in fact, it became her to the manner born. And—thought Betty, with a thrill of pride—what a Countess she would make! His lordship was a lucky man, indeed!

The bedroom door opened, and Amelia hurried in, a glittering vision in rose and silver, with diamonds on her bosom, on her wrists, in her hair. Her gloves and her slippers had come from France, and exactly matched the gauzy cloud of delicate tulle of which her gown was made. Her hair was elaborately dressed and her complexion tinted with consummate art. She looked very beautiful and quite artificial. Betty, comparing her ladyship with the glowing creature standing before the mirror, privately thought that Lady Carfax looked rather common—like an opera-dancer, or one of those light ladies; so thought loyal Betty, looking at them both.

Amelia, however, was in high gig; well satisfied with her appearance, and transported into a positively beatific mood by the compliments and congratulations that had been showered upon her on the occasion of her niece's engagement. As though, Betty thought resentfully, she had had something to do with Miss Bethesda's success—which she hadn't, not her.

'Now, my dear, are you ready to go down?' She smiled brilliantly, her china-blue eyes sparkling. 'Everyone is waiting. I shall go down first, and you follow. Come, really, this is very exciting! I am sure I do not know when I enjoyed anything so much! And I must say—that gown is most successful. Yes, indeed; you look very pleasing . . . And now we must delay no longer. Come along, Bethesda!'

In the gallery above the great flagged hall, the musicians were softly playing. At either end of the wide apartment, massive logs burned in the huge stone fireplaces; and hundreds of candles flamed on the walls and overhead, sending light to the farthest corner. Marcus stood with Lord Carfax and a group of gentlemen in evening dress; he was chatting with smiling ease, and acknowledging the greetings of various acquaintances; but from the corner of his eye he was watching the stairs.

Amelia came smiling around the long curve of the flight, secure in the knowledge that she was looking her best; and well pleased with herself as well as—for the time being—with her niece. Her rose-coloured skirts whispered over the carpeted treads and her diamonds threw back the light in a thousand facets. But as a shimmer of white appeared behind her, heads turned, and eyes went past her ladyship; to fasten, in amazement and a sort of homage, on the girl following in Amelia's wake.

A hush fell over the guests. One by one, their voices died away, as they faced about to watch the Viscount's chosen bride descend the stairs. A little smile curved her red mouth, and her eyes glowed as deep as the emerald in the betrothal ring which Marcus had placed on her finger that very morning. The satin dress flowed over her long limbs like water, and her skin seemed translucent and lit from within; as if she imparted, rather than reflected light, gliding down the staircase in a kind of luminosity. In years to come, she was on many occasions to startle an assembled company into attention, when she made her entrance; but she was never to look more beautiful than she did on that night, as she walked down the stairs to Marcus—just as she had done on the first, the very first occasion that they had met; down to the bottom stair—exactly the same—meeting his eyes across the intervening space . . . But this time—how different!

Bethesda tingled all over with joyousness, with glorious exhilaration. The future stretched before her, unblemished by a single cloud. Was it wrong to be so happy? A tiny shiver went over her; she gave herself a mental shake. Nothing, ever, could possibly spoil this happiness!

She reached the lowest stair; and the Viscount stepped forward to meet her.

CHAPTER
SIX

MARCUS and Bethesda were married in the old church at
Ansteys where her parents had exchanged their vows
before the ancient altar. Amelia had hoped for a
fashionable wedding in town, with all the pomp and
ceremony possible. The most sought-after matrimonial
prize in London was marrying a girl straight from the
schoolroom; Amelia had looked forward to the gnashing
of teeth and the envious whispers of all the match-
making mamas who had cast their lures for the Viscount,
and the forward damsels who had set their caps at him.
In vain did she point out to the young people the
inconvenience of accommodating wedding guests in the
country, the state of the roads for travelling—for winter
lingered, and the byways were hard frosted—the incon-
siderateness of their behaviour in causing dear Lady
Cumnor to come to the depths of the country just to suit
their whim. Marcus, in that annoyingly firm tone of his,
assured her that his mother would travel comfortably in
the Earl's great travelling-coach, which was fitted with
every modern luxury; and Bethesda took courage to
inform her aunt that it was her unshakeable resolve to be
married in the church as her parents had been. Faced
with their united determination, Amelia had to give in,
and retired with a sick headache to lie in her darkened
bedroom, prophesying to her lord that none of those

invited to the ceremony would brave the muddy roads, and that those who did would meet with disaster on the way.

In this she was mistaken. A goodly number of friends, who remembered the bride's parents with affection, came to see Carfax's girl married, and to wish her well. The weather held frosty and still, with a pale watery sun to dispel the mists that clung round the old stone walls. Lord and Lady Cumnor duly arrived, followed by their baggage coach, after an uneventful journey. Constance, accompanying them, was to be Bethesda's only bridesmaid. Bethesda awaited the sound of carriage wheels on the gravel driveway, and hurried down to greet her friend. The heavy front door swung open, and Constance, swathed in furs, her little nose pink from cold, and her soft eyes sparkling, came in with a rush and flung her arms around Bethesda's neck.

'Bethy, I am so happy!' she cried. 'It is just what I wished for! When Mama told me I was so delighted; we shall be sisters!'

The next moment, the Viscount, Lord Carfax and Amelia entered the great hall, just as Lady Cumnor, followed by the Earl, made her entrance. In spite of two days of travelling, Marcus's stately mother retained her air of calm and her immaculate appearance. Bethesda, rising from her obeisance to her future mama-in-law, felt her hand taken in a firm clasp; the lady's deep blue eyes, so like her son's, were smiling; she patted Bethesda's hand, and said, kindly,

'I was surprised, my dear, when Marcus confided to me that he had lost his heart. But I am well pleased. Your Mama and I were school-friends; and presently, when I am rested, I look forward to a long talk with you.'

Lady Cumnor, accompanied by a nervous Amelia—for she was secretly in awe of the Countess—then retired to the suite of rooms set aside for her. Lord Cumnor, a thickset gentleman with grey twinkling eyes, accompanied Lord Carfax into the library, where decanters were set out before a welcoming fire. Marcus, at a nod from his sire, went with them; the door closed and the two girls were left alone. Hand in hand, they flew up the great stairs like two swallows, followed by the indulgent smile of Mrs Wirth the housekeeper and Evans, the Carfax butler. Mrs Wirth remarked that it was a pleasure to see Miss Bethesda so happy, and the butler, who remembered quite well the morning when their young lady had been sent away, weeping, to school, agreed in his stately manner that it was indeed.

Constance and Bethesda collapsed together on the huge four-poster in the Blue Room, which had been set aside for the bridesmaid's use.

'Oh!' Constance gasped. 'If Mama could see me run up the stairs! But I am so excited, Bethy! You and Marcus—it is perfect!'

The wedding day dawned frosty and still, but the guests in the old Norman church were snug enough. Braziers warmed the stone interior, with its tall windows and strong pillars. The voices of the village choir rose to the dim ceiling; and many of the local people who remembered the 'real' lord and his lady, ventured out with nipping fingers and toes to see their own young miss be married. Opinion was divided among the local matrons as to which made the prettier bride; Bethesda or her mother. 'Fair as a hedge-rose her mother was,' said an old beldame, standing with her cronies in the churchyard, waiting for the young couple to appear. 'And his lordship, so strong and bold, with his hair like a raven's wing. Ah, dearie me, it's a sad thing that they can't see her married; and I'm sure I wish her and her gentleman very happy.'

A murmur of agreement arose. Then the bells pealed out, the church door opened, and the wedding party emerged. A cheer went up from the waiting crowd, for there was not one among them who did not wish her well. Gasps of admiration were heard at sight of the bride, a radiant goddess in satin and lace, and her mother's delicate diamond necklace. Her veil fell in a pearly shower to her feet, and her hair glinted through it even in the misty light. The Viscount was a sight that drew a sigh from the breasts of several staid farmers' wives, who had thought themselves immune to the effects of masculine beauty. His lordship's morning coat of black superfine fitted like a glove to his superb shoulders and narrow waist; elegant pantaloons of dove grey encased his muscular legs; his golden curls, bare to the raw morning mist, curled crisply on his forehead. Half the damsels in the village fell instant victim to the sapphire glance of his smiling eyes, as he gazed around at the onlookers. Constance, following, won her share of compliments. A real little lady, was the general verdict, gentle and sweet, as anyone could see from the soft expression of her face, framed in a pink satin bonnet that exactly matched the rich gleaming folds of her velvet-trimmed gown. She carried a posy of pink hothouse roses, and looked, it was agreed, as pretty as a rose herself.

After a few minutes, the Viscountess whispered to her husband, and they turned aside together, moving along a side path. Her skirts swept the frozen gravel and the cold struck through her satin shoes, but she took no heed. In a minute or two they were standing before the family vault. Here lay generations of Carfaxes with their wedded wives beside them. A Carfax who had crusaded with Richard was here, his mailed hands forever clasped in effigy on his breast. A cavalier Carfax who fell under the banner of the first Charles slept through eternity not far away. Bethesda entered the quiet edifice and laid her white bouquet beside the newest coffins. She stood for a moment, silent, in the deathly cold. Then she turned back to Marcus, and together they walked to where the carriages stood by the churchyard gate. The horses' breath steamed; their hooves rang on the iron-hard ground; and back to Ansteys went the wedding guests, where the bridal feast, laid out in the enormous dining room, awaited their attention.

Many hours later, when the music, feasting and dancing were done, and the guests had either been sped on their way or lighted to their bedchambers for the night, a deep silence settled on the old house. Low dark clouds, borne on the back of the nightwind, came rolling across the midland country and hung over the old black chimneys, as the keen airs sang about them. Bethesda and her love, hidden away in the silence, enveloped by the thick walls, the heavy curtains drawn, the firelight casting light and shadows on the carved ceiling, lay in each other's arms; and were lost in the glory of their own private world. Outside, softly, a few white flakes of late-falling snow floated like a blessing past the shuttered windows.

It was ten o'clock on a fine London morning, and the steps in front of Lord Cumnor's imposing town residence had already been scrubbed and whitened by a diligent housemaid, who was not however too busy to exchange some lively remarks with a butcher's boy who went whistling down the street. Inside, the kitchens of the huge house were full of bustle and savoury smells, for breakfast was completed in the servants' hall and the nursery, and preparations were in full swing for the descent of the family to the breakfast-parlour. Lady Cumnor had never succumbed to the habit of breakfasting in bed. Eleven o'clock would find her enthroned behind the coffee urn, ready to pour out his breakfast coffee for her lord, as he sat reading the morning journals that had been carefully smoothed with a flatiron before the butler presented them on a silver tray.

In their sumptuous suite of rooms on the third floor, however, the Viscount and his bride had been graciously excused from the breakfast ritual. Some lassitude must be allowed to a couple so newly married. Handing a steaming cup to her husband, Lady Cumnor reflected that it was surprising that Bethesda did not sleep the clock round, when one considered the stream of invitations that had been showered upon Marcus's wife from the moment she had appeared in town. Lady Mainwaring's beauty was already the toast of the ton; gilt-edged missives arrived by every post; posies, sonnets, pretty trifles of all sorts, were delivered daily by a growing tribe of rapturous admirers; they extolled her eyes as emerald stars, compared her hair to the sunset; she was a goddess, a Juno, a swaying willow, a gliding swan; in short, Bethesda had become the rage. The town buzzed with the charms of the newest beauty. Certain spiteful females who declared her too tall for perfection, and suggested that her hair must owe its colour to art not nature, were not attended to. Lady Cumnor, sipping her

coffee, admitted to herself that she privately agreed with
Nurse's expressed opinion; it was fortunate that Constance was only just sixteen, and that her coming-out ball
would not take place until next season. Devoted mother
though she was, Lady Cumnor realised that Bethesda's
looks cast Constance in the shade. Fortunately, it was
not a problem. Bethesda could reign as society's darling
for the present; by next year, Lady Cumnor hoped—
with fond anticipation—the Viscountess would be increasing, in which case she would retire to Yorkshire to
await her confinement. The Countess looked forward
with deep pleasure to the arrival of her first grandchild.
In the meantime, the lady was happy in the happiness of
the newly-weds.

Up on the third floor of the mansion, Bethesda lay in
bed, stretching luxuriously, and reached her hand for
the morning chocolate which had just been brought in by
a soft-footed maid, who then stepped to the windows
and drew open the velvet curtains with their heavy silver
edging. Marcus had had his bride's bedchamber hung
with palest green and silver. A cloud of gauze constituted the bed curtains and silver cupids dimpled at the
corners of the huge four-poster, above ruched valances
of apple green silk. The adjoining boudoir was a sym-
phony of amber and gold, with gilded mirrors on every
wall, and a gilt escritoire in the window bay, where her
ladyship might answer at her leisure some of the pile of
letters and cards that spilled off her breakfast tray.

Still flushed with sleep, the Viscountess extended her
arms for the froth of cascading frills that comprised her
morning robe, and looked up as the door opened. The
Viscount entered, resplendent in a frogged dressing-
gown of ruby silk, which became him remarkably well.

He held a letter in his hand, and as he regarded his bride, a mischievous smile crept over his mouth.

'Good-morning, love,' he said, 'I do hope you slept well?'

Bethesda blushed, and the dimple near her mouth deepened. The maid withdrew noiselessly, and the Viscountess, meeting her lord and master's teasing gaze, pushed her tray aside and held out her arms. Caught against his hard chest, she hid her face on his silken shoulder, and said in a muffled voice,

'Indeed, my lord, I slept but little, as well you know!'

'Are you tired, my darling?' he asked, smoothing her hair with a gentle hand.

'No, not at all,' she said, with a tiny laugh, 'and Marcus, I do love you so!' She lifted her hand to touch his face, resting a finger-tip on the tiny mole beside his mouth, tracing lightly along the smooth line of his lips. At her touch, his arms tightened into iron bands, and a blue gleam shone between his narrowed lids; their mouths met, burning one into the other; she sank back on the pillows, her bones turning to water, her flesh dissolving into his.

'My lady, this will never do,' said the Viscount some little time later, running a hand through his tousled locks, and increasing, if possible, their disarray. 'Behave yourself, witch, and sit on my knee; but keep still, madam, or it will.be the worse for you! I came to talk to you, and talk I mean to do!'

'Yes, dear Marcus,' she said demurely, and subsided on his lap, head pillowed on his chest. Squinting a little through the cloud of hair that was obscuring his vision, the Viscount held up the letter he had brought, so that they might read it together.

'You see, love, where Horton writes that my signature is required for the lease of the water-meadows, and also there are some matters of tenancy to be settled,' he pointed out. 'It means that I must spend a few days in Yorkshire. Horton cannot handle these matters on his own.'

'Of course not,' she agreed. 'I have no objection, my lord. When would you wish us to leave?'

'Do you mean that you will accompany me?' he asked with pleased surprise. 'I am afraid it will be dull for you, love; I shall be occupied with business for most of the day; and then—' he gestured to the cards and letters that were, by now, scattered willy-nilly over the carpet. 'What about all your engagements? Can you break them heartlessly?' In shocked tones, he continued, 'And what of your admirers? Do you mean to desert them all so cruelly? Shame on you, madam! Why, half the beaux in London will put an end to their existence if the Incomparable is not to be seen for a week!'

'How absurd you are!' said his wife, giggling. 'Be very sure I shall accompany you, my lord. Do you think I would let you out of my sight? I would never dare! I should be afraid that some designing female would snatch you up to her bosom—and then, perhaps, you might prefer her charms to mine—' She got no further, for the Viscount stopped her mouth with his own, and the conversation came to a sudden end. Taking his leave of her some time later, the Viscount informed his wife that she had cast doubt on his fidelity as a lover, but he hoped that he had set her mind at rest. He then departed, after promising himself the pleasure of riding with her ladyship in the park in the afternoon; and retired to his own rooms, to be shaved and dressed, before joining some friends for a work-out at Jackson's boxing saloon.

Bethesda lay full length among the tumbled bed-covers, arms flung over her head, bathed in a glow of contentment. Her mouth was bruised from his kisses; she quivered still from the touch of his hands. Gradually, a dreamy quietness stole over her, enfolding body and mind; she drew a deep breath of happiness, turned into the pillows, and drifted off into sleep. She did not stir until the maidservant returned, at one o'clock, to en-quire if her ladyship would require some luncheon.

Later that afternoon, young Lady Mainwaring, escorted by her husband, was to be seen mounted on Nightbird, trotting sedately through the park where daffodils nodded along the grassy verges, and winter branches were showing the green of spring. It was absolutely obligatory, in the world of fashion, to be seen in the park, riding, driving, or even walking, at the hour of five o'clock. Various sporting ladies dashed by, driv-ing phaetons, behind high-stepping teams; a goodly number of elegantly clad ladies and gentlemen were strolling about; a number of others were showing their paces on horseback; but none could surpass the grace and style of the young Viscountess. She wore a sculp-tured habit of pale blue cloth, and her curls clustered under a black satin tophat, set straight above the eyes, with a white veil flowing away behind her. Catching sight of a well-known figure in the distance, she said,

'Marcus, there are Constance and Miss Hartigan, just arrived. Let us go and meet them.' Side by side, they cantered towards the gates, where Constance and the governess were in the act of alighting from the family barouche.

'My lord!' exclaimed her ladyship, as they drew near, 'I have such a splendid idea! If she would like it, let us take Connie with us to Yorkshire! We will be company for each other, while you are closeted with your agent; and you know she loves to ride free upon the moors, just as I do!'

This suggestion was warmly approved by Marcus, and arriving where Constance stood with the governess, was immediately proffered. Constance accepted with delight. A bout of influenza had postponed her return to Miss Skeffington's, and, relegated to the schoolroom, she was finding the days rather tedious. She did not complain, being much too sweet-tempered, but the prospect of a week in the relative freedom of the family estates offered a welcome change. If Mama consented, she said happily, and surely there was no reason she should not, Constance would gladly accompany them.

None of the party happened to notice a tall gentleman, excessively elegant, who stood watching them from the shelter of a spreading tree a short distance away. Leaning on his amber cane, one shoulder propped against the trunk, he was apparently engrossed in observing the passers-by. Only a very close observer might have wondered at something fixed and motionless in the gentleman's regard, and at the tension of his gloved fist clenched on the handle of the cane. If they had looked even more carefully, they might have seen the savage twist of his thin mouth, and the ugly light in his eyes, under the shadow of the curly-brimmed beaver that was set upon his well-groomed head.

CHAPTER
SEVEN

THE journey to Yorkshire was accomplished by easy
stages. The Viscount's post-chaise was well-sprung,
well-cushioned, and carefully lined against creeping
draughts. The weather was fairly mild as they took the
great North road, with their respective maid and valet
following in the second coach, baggage strapped to its
roof. As they went further north, however, it began to
rain, and the air became dank and cold. But inside the
chaise they were comfortable enough; and the smart
posting-inns along the road offered blazing fires, private
parlours, and well-aired sheets to those travellers who
were rich enough to pay their prices. Lady Constance
and the Viscount pointed out to Bethesda such places of
interest as were to be seen along the way, and when the
landscape became hidden by grey driving rain, his
lordship, long legs stretched out and fair head resting on
the velvet squabs, entertained his two companions with
humorous anecdotes and snatches of song delivered in a
resounding baritone. As the miles fell away behind, the
Viscount set himself to amuse them both, and on several
occasions the two girls collapsed in helpless giggles at his
nonsense. The road to home, Constance thought,
seemed shorter than it ever had before.

None of them was aware of the man who followed
them through the long journey, carefully keeping one

stage behind. His heart smouldered with an ugly jealous rage, and his brain had become obsessed. He was, indeed, almost past rational thought, so bitter had his mind become. He could not rest, and his head was filled with one thought only; revenge. She had made a fool of him, and she was going to pay. He would be revenged; he could think no farther than that. And as they went north, deeper and deeper into the remote countryside, he continued to follow them.

Ribston, Lord Cumnor's family seat, stood on a sheltered rise, with its back to the bleak hills. The huge grey pile, added to over the centuries, sprawled across a four-hundred-foot frontage. Before it, a great sweep of lawn flanked by a fine topiary garden rolled down to the edge of the icy lake, where the sharp wind sent steely ripples across the black surface. To the north, the wild moors stretched away. The house itself was surrounded by a spacious park, whose trees had been planted and nurtured by the long-dead forbear who rode into battle with his liege lord, known to his friends—and enemies— as the Black Prince. His Highness had bestowed the demesne of Ribston upon his loyal knight; and there the Earls of Cumnor had remained, although there were other family properties in their possession, including the dark and draughty stone tower in Northumberland from which the family had originally sprung, at some far-off date back in the mists of time.

It was dusk as the travellers approached, and the great gates were opened for the Viscount's carriage. A half-mile of driveway led up through the dark trees. The chaise swept under the arched gate tower and into a cobbled courtyard, where the castle walls soared steeply above, into the freezing sky. And here were lights, open doors, smiling servants, warmth and welcome. The carriage steps were let down, the travellers hurried inside; the front door with its huge iron studs closed behind them. Within, there was bustle and cheer, and love and laughter. Outside, the wintry dark closed in again, and settled into silence.

Entering the panelled library of Ribston, where the dark walls and tall bookshelves were lit by firelight, the two young ladies found Marcus, foot on fender, staring into the flames. Both girls glowed with cold and exercise, although Constance admitted that she did not have Bethy's passion for wild weather and freezing winds; she preferred the warmth of summer. Bethesda, however, had taken to the bracing climate of Yorkshire with enthusiasm, and already a deep affection for the estate had grown in her. She loved Ansteys still; but already Ribston had become her home. Marcus looked up smiling, as Constance exclaimed,

'We have had such a gallop! It was glorious! We struck across Whinstanes, and came down along the spur, skirting the old quarry; you know the way, Marcus, it is one of my favourite rides. Bethy will soon know every foot of the estate! I showed her the dangerous place, where the bushes hide the quarry edge.'

'I hope you did not outrun your groom, kitten,' said her brother. 'I know what a bruising rider you are; And Bethy is even more reckless. I want to be sure that Martin has you both in sight, wherever you go. It's lonely countryside hereabouts.'

'Yes, love, we were very good,' answered Bethesda, coming forward to the fireplace. 'I would not cause you any worry, for the world—you know that! Couldn't you

join us to-morrow, Marcus? I should like it of all things!'
and her hand found his.

'As it happens,' he answered, pressing her fingers
warmly, 'I mean to drive over to-morrow to speak with
Tyson. I thought, Bethy, you might like to come with
me. We will take the curricle, and you can handle the
ribbons.'

She was about to agree, happily; and then a thought
struck her.

'We leave the day after to-morrow, and Connie has to
return to school,' she pointed out. 'Let her go driving
with you; she loves to drive the curricle, and I will have
many more chances to do so, after she is back at the
Seminary.'

'Would you like that, love?' Marcus asked his sister.

'Indeed, yes,' said Constance, 'if you are sure, Bethy,
that you don't mind. But what will you do? We cannot all
three go in a curricle, and you will be alone, with nothing
to occupy you.'

'I mean to be well occupied,' said Bethesda, moving
closer to her lord, and sending him a brilliant slanting
glance beneath her lashes. 'I will go riding again; but
to-morrow I will ride Storm King.'

'The devil you will!' exclaimed the Viscount, startled.
'Now, listen, ma'am; just wait one moment, if you
please—'

'Oh, Marcus, you know I can manage him,' pleaded
his wife, her face raised to his. 'You said yourself that I
manage him as well as a man; and you said—'

'Never mind what I said!' objected her harassed husband. 'That was different, I was with you, and we went
only through the park!'

'But if Martin comes with me? On the chestnut? I

would be quite safe, and I promise not to try any dangerous jumps. Oh, Marcus, please! I would like it so much! You know, Papa was wont to mount me on his hunters, even before I could walk!'

He hesitated. It was true; he had never seen a better rider, and she had handled the stallion with perfect ease. Moreover, the King, for all his stature and strength, was sweet-tempered and without vice. Although so powerful a horse was not really a lady's mount, still—Bethesda was no ordinary lady.

'Very well,' he said at last, 'But you must stay with Martin. I just can't bear to think of any hurt befalling you. And keep away from the quarry cliff; there have been rockfalls, there, and the edge is steep and dangerous.'

'Thank you, my lord!' she said happily. 'I will take care of the King! Trust me not to ruin his mouth!'

'In truth,' he admitted, with a reluctant grin, 'I can think of no other pair of hands, man or woman, to whom I would sooner entrust him.'

Dimpling, she bobbed him a curtsey, and turning to Constance, she said, 'come, little sister, we are mud to the eyebrows, and must make ourselves presentable before we dine.' She threw him a kiss, and a saucy backward look, as the two girls left the room together.

So it came about that on the following afternoon, Bethesda waved good-bye to her husband and Constance, perched side by side on the curricle box. The air was cold and damp, and Constance was muffled to the eyebrows, in a warm cloak buttoned to the throat, and a close bonnet which hid her hair. Little more than the tip of her nose could be seen. Her small hands in leather gloves did not look strong enough to handle the matched bays that were clouding the air with their breath, but she was in fact an accomplished whip; and the bays, their heads released, swept off in dashing style around the gravelled curve, and were soon lost to sight behind the trees bordering the avenue.

In a moment, Martin came into sight, mounted on the chestnut. A young groom followed, leading Storm King. Her heart lifted as she looked at the mighty grey; she loved her hack Nightbird dearly, but he was stabled in London, and to gallop free on King's back, borne on the wings of his strength and speed, was a prospect that could not fail to please a girl who had ridden horseback before she could walk. The groom extended his cupped hands; she vaulted into the saddle; and they were off.

The avenue was shadowy, and the King danced sideways as a small creature stirred in the undergrowth; he reared up as a hare scuttled across the path, and Martin urged forward to catch at the reins, but it was unnecessary; her ladyship never shifted in her seat, and Martin breathed again, and followed her, his master's parting admonitions ringing in his ears. Soon they were through the home wood, and out on the open moor; and she gave the stallion his head. They raced away. The thud of King's hoofs shook the earth; the wind sang in her ears. It seemed to her that together they could fly off the earth's rim, and soar above the clouds. Glowing and exhilarated, she reined in at last, easing King to a canter, to allow Martin to come up with them. The chestnut was a rare goer, but he could not match the stallion stride for stride.

'How I enjoyed that!' she called to the groom. 'What a splendid creature he is, Martin!' She patted King's neck. 'Which way should we go, do you think?'

'Well, my lady, we could follow up Ribston Spur to the high moor, where there's a good safe galloping; and then drop down towards Tyson's, and canter back along the home road. There's a good chance we might meet his lordship returning; and we could accompany them home.'

'Capital!' she said, and gathered up the reins. 'What a good plan! We will do just as you say, and very likely strike them in the avenue, on our way back. Come, then!'

'Now don't you go and lose me, my lady,' warned the groom, 'or his lordship'll have my hide, so he promised me!'

By the time that the route outlined by Martin was covered, and they dropped down at last into the home wood, the afternoon was well advanced. The outcrops of rugged stone were outlined against a grey sky. Martin squinted at the darkening horizon, and said, 'I think his lordship may be past the crossroads by now, m'lady,' and added, 'I know he did not mean to stay above an hour or so at Tyson's. We had best press on home. His lordship would not wish you to be out after dark, ma'am.'

'Let us cut across the fields towards the avenue,' Bethesda said. 'We may come up with them there, after all.'

At a brisk trot they made their way across several meadows, skirting various patches of early turnips and oats, and presently found themselves among the trees, approaching the long avenue that led away to the house. A bridle path led them through the forest, and as they breasted a grassy knoll overlooking the avenue, the sound of horses' hooves was heard. Pointing with his riding-crop along the darkening vista, Martin said,

'Here comes his lordship now, ma'am, and Lady Constance driving. Very well she handles them too.'

'Yes, indeed,' Bethesda said. 'Let us go and meet them.'

In the dusk the curricle swept around a long curve, with Constance holding the bays well up to their bits. Beside her, Marcus was seated, his thoughts ranging over the afternoon just past, and the satisfactory outcome of the discussion with his tenant. Constance had been warmly welcomed by Mrs Tyson, taken into the parlour, and regaled with home-made currant wine; an hour had swiftly passed while Constance replied to the good lady's questions regarding the welfare of her Mama, brother and sisters; and a promise given that on the very next visit to the farm, Marcus's bride should accompany them. 'Mrs Tyson said that everyone is exclaiming over Bethy's beauty, and calling you a lucky man,' Constance informed her brother, with a twinkling sideways glance.

'I know it,' said Marcus simply. 'When she ain't with me, I miss her every moment. I just hope, love, that you will be as fortunate yourself, one day, and that we find a rattling good fellow, worthy of you, who will make you truly happy.'

'I am sure I hope so too,' answered his sister laughing, 'but in the meantime, I am happy for you both. Bethy is perfect for you.'

Her words were scarcely uttered when a shot rang out; fired, it seemed to her brother, from over the horses' very heads. The bays surged wildly forward, panic-stricken; before Marcus could fully take in what had occurred, the reins slipped from Constance's hands and went slack. He snatched at them desperately; the horses were bolting. With a thrill of incredulous horror he realised that Constance had slumped forward on the seat, head sagging, face hidden. The curricle rocked crazily, and for an agonised moment he thought she would fall. He clamped one arm around her limp body, and legs braced against the footboard, reins gripped in his free hand, he fought to bring the terrified horses under control. Suddenly he felt a spreading warmth on his hand, and with a sick fear saw that his sister was bleeding. Of the extent of her hurt he had no idea, but certainly she was hit, and hit badly; she seemed unconscious. The miscreant who had fired the shot—careless poacher, or whoever he might be—would have to wait. Ashen-faced, the Viscount was aware only of the desperate urgency of getting his sister back to the house.

Coming from the trees on to the little rise above them, Bethesda saw the whole thing. The bays swept into the distance, but not before she saw Constance sag forward, apparently fainting. Across the avenue, from where the shot had come, a shadow darker than the rest resolved itself into a furtive movement. In another moment, her ears caught the muffled sound of hooves on the leafy mould underfoot.

Bethesda uttered an oath that her Papa had been known to use on the hunting-field. She drove her spurs into the stallion's sides and with a tremendous leap Storm King cleared the bank, bounded across the road and plunged into the woods on the other side.

Hanging low on the horse's neck, she urged him through the woods at full gallop. Her keen eyes could just make out the fleeing figure ahead as they raced under the spreading branches. She could not see his face; but a sick conviction gripped her. It must be—it had to be—Barrington. Barrington, a deadly marksman, never beaten in a duel, who had waited for his revenge, and had mistaken Constance for herself. Even in the dim light, he had not missed his mark.

Only—he had hit Constance instead, and even now—even now, her little sister whom she loved, might be badly hurt; might be . . . dead.

Through the woods the riders flew. Barrington glanced over his shoulder and saw that his pursuer was gaining on him. He swore, dragged his horse's head round and headed for the open. If he gained the spur, he could get away across the moors; in the falling darkness he would soon be lost to sight. He cursed the unlucky chance that had provided his crime with a witness. He had thought the woods deserted. But once upon the moor he would be safe enough. Hobden was waiting with his curricle in a high-hedged secluded lane, and when they were safely away from this place the blame could never be fastened on him. His guilt would never be proved.

He would never have the Carfax heiress; but Mainwaring, may he rot in hell, would not have her either.

Bethesda saw him change direction, and eased King's pace a little. The line he was following would take him along the lip of the old quarry. A sudden plan flashed through her mind. If she cut across the fields, bore in on his flank, and he turned to the right—! Her full lips were set in a grim line. Her eyes shone like polished stones between narrowed lids. Her face was hard and expressionless. With cold deadly fury in her heart, her whole being frozen into single-minded purpose, she turned King's head. As Barrington raced for his life up the long rising slope that skirted the quarry's edge, Bethesda thundered out from the trees, the stallion's hooves pounding, a living vengeance, bearing inescapably down upon him. From the corner of his eye he saw the approaching rider, and he turned to the right, urging his sweating horse up the slope.

Hair streaming, teeth gritted, eyes blazing, she hunted him like a fox, closer and closer to that treacherous edge where the bushes grew. Up the long rocky slope he raced, through the low brush that masked the sudden sheer drop into the depths below.

His horse, in desperate fear, sensed the danger and screamed shrilly; reared up; and teetered on the very brink. At the last second, when it seemed too late, the frantic animal wheeled, white-eyed; scrabbled and plunged madly on the loose stones; and crashed heavily down on its side. Barrington, thrown clear, rolled among flying earth and pebbles, over and over, to the sheer edge of the drop, and lay stunned. The horse, nostrils wide and flanks heaving, scrambled to its feet and galloped some little distance away down the hill; then it pulled up short, and stood dazed, blowing and trembling.

Groaning and cursing, Barrington groped his way to a sitting position, head in hands; and looked up, to see, poised above him on the stallion's back, the girl who was watching him, quite still, with dead-white face and eyes like daggers. Open-mouthed, he lurched to his feet, staring, eyes starting from their sockets. In a whisper like the hissing of a snake, she spoke, very low; but the words reached his ears.

'Constance,' she said. 'It was Constance.'

He broke into a stream of curses. Shouting and swearing he reached into his pocket and dragged out a pistol. One of the pair had already been fired; this other would do for her. With an obscenity in his mouth, and seething madness in his brain, he levelled the weapon.

In the same moment that he pulled the trigger the stallion reared madly. Its nostrils flared; its piercing cry rang shrilly in his brain. Before the menace of those plunging forehooves, he reeled backwards, and the shot went wide. Again King reared, high above his head, and for a moment, the three of them, girl, horse and man, were poised in silhouette against the sky.

The flying hooves lunged down again; a heavy blow caught him on the shoulder. He flung up his arms— staggered—and went over the edge.

He gave one shriek as he careened downwards, bouncing from rock to rock, rolling towards the valley below. Then his skull smashed upon a jutting crag; and all was silent.

Bethesda sat on King's back, staring at the place where Barrington had disappeared. She did not move nor speak. They stood there, the girl and the great white horse, while the last light died away. The riderless horse, a little way off, began, quietly, to crop the grass.

She did not move when Martin, panting and sweating, came up at last to the cliff's edge, and reined in beside her. She only said, without turning her head,

'Bring the horse, if you please.' Then she gathered the reins, stroked King's neck, and turned his head for home. They rode, silent, back through the night; through the home wood; along the avenue; to where the house awaited them, with windows alight in the misty dark. A thin cold rain had begun to fall; it stung their faces as they rode on.

At the front door a strange carriage stood, with a dark-clad groom holding the horses' heads. Bethesda slid from King's back, handed the reins to Martin; and began to mount the stone stairs to the front door. Before she could lift her hand to the heavy knocker the door swung open, and she was confronted with the anguished faces of the butler and housekeeper. Mrs Bailey was wringing her hands; tears were pouring down her face.

'Oh, my lady, I don't know how to tell you,' she wailed. 'Our young lady is shot—by a poacher, they say; and she's mortal bad; dying, they say—the doctor's with her, and his lordship; they've stopped the bleeding, but Nurse heard Doctor say she's sinking, and they haven't got the bullet out. And oh, the good lord, that such a thing should come upon us!' and the poor soul, giving in to her feelings, buried her face in her apron and ran away down the hall towards the servants' quarters.

White as a graven image, Bethesda spoke to the butler.

'Send my maid to me, please,' and slowly, like a sleep-walker, she mounted the stairs. When a red-eyed Betty arrived, she found her mistress, stony-eyed, seated at the dressing-table.

'I am going to retire to bed,' said the Vicountess. 'Tell his lordship that I am too overcome by this terrible tragedy to see anybody to-night. I wish to be left entirely alone. Now leave me.'

'But, Miss—your ladyship—' Betty began.

'Do as I say! Tell his lordship that I am prostrated with shock, and wish to be alone. Tell him—' her voice quivered—'tell him that I shall see him in the morning. Now go!'

'Very well, my lady,' said Betty, and withdrew.

As the door shut behind the maid, Bethesda rose, and crossing to the bed, she lifted the bolster and arranged it lengthwise under the covers. She tumbled the pillows and drew the bed-curtains close. From the wardrobe, she selected a dark wool gown, cloak and close-fitting bonnet. Her riding clothes were bundled into the bottom of the wardrobe. A modest selection of linen and toilet articles went quickly into a single small bandbox. She thrust her purse into the deep pocket of her cloak. On the bedside chest were her writing materials. She snuffed out all but a solitary candle, and in the semi-dark, her eyes shadowed by their heavy lashes, she penned a note.

'My dearest love,' she wrote steadily, 'when you read this I shall be far away. It is my Fault that this awful thing has happened. I have brought trouble upon you all. Barrington is dead. Martin will tell you the whole. Goodbye, my beloved husband. Bethesda.'

On top of the paper she placed her wedding ring and the glowing emerald betrothal ring that Marcus had given her. She propped the letter against the mirror; blew out the last candle, and opened the door.

No one was there to see her as she walked down the staircase, across the hall, and out of the house. Had the butler returned from the kitchen regions a minute sooner, he must surely have intercepted her; but as it was, on finding the front door unfastened, he merely blamed his own troubled state of mind for the oversight, and fastened and locked it firmly. Even the doctor's groom was no longer in the driveway; the groom had only that moment taken the carriage around to the stables. No one happened to be watching, even from the upper windows, as she crossed the drive, traversed the lawn, and came to the woods. The next minute, she was lost to sight, as her tall figure muffled in the cloak merged into the darkness of the trees.

Marcus stood at the foot of his sister's bed. Her small face, whiter than the pillows, was closed like a sleeping flower. Her slim body barely moulded the bedclothes; her breathing hardly lifted her slight breast. He gripped the bedrail, white-knuckled, as he watched her face, willing the eyelids to flicker, the lips to move. Beyond the circle of light, Nurse moved quietly, removing blood-stained cloths, a basin of reddened water, some scraps of lint that had fallen to the carpet. Closing his bag, the doctor, a trim little man with needle-sharp eyes, pursed his lips, stepped quietly back, and beckoned to his lordship.

'The bullet came out clean, my lord, and missed the lung,' he said, 'but she's lost a lot of blood. So I shan't bleed her, as the wound is clean, and there's no fever. Now, we can only wait and see if she rallies. I'll be off now, and come back at dawn. If she stirs, try to give her some of the saline draught. If she worsens, send the boy for me. I'll come at once.'

'Will she live?' asked Marcus in husky tones.

'As to that, much depends on her constitution,' replied the doctor briefly. 'The pulse is very weak, and extracting the bullet has tried her strength sorely. Keep her warm; try to get her to drink; I'll return in the morning.' He gave a brief bow, picked up his bag, and after a low word of instruction to the nurse, left the room.

Marcus placed a chair beside the bed, and sat down, his eyes on Constance's face. A great weariness swept over him, and more than anything else, he longed for the

strong slim hand of Bethesda in his own, to share the
long hours of desperate waiting ahead. Still watching his
sister's face, he beckoned to Nurse, and said,

'Has her ladyship come in yet?'

'I will enquire, my lord,' was the reply, and nurse
moved softly to the door. There was a brief whispered
conversation, and the woman returned to the bed.

'Her ladyship's maid wishes to speak with you,' she
whispered.

He rose and went to the door, where the anxious face
of Betty awaited him. As he took in the sense of her
low-voiced message from Bethesda, a pang of puzzled
disappointment that his love should absent herself from
his side at such a time, and in such circumstances, shot
through his mind; and was instantly dismissed. It was
understandable, he told himself; she was overwhelmed
by shock and grief; she could not face the ordeal of
seeing Constance. He would not blame her for a single
moment.

'Where is your mistress now?' he asked.

'Resting in her bed, with the curtains drawn, my lord,'
came the answer. 'I looked in, but a moment ago; the
candles are all put out, and the curtains drawn. She must
be deep asleep, sir, for I could not even hear her
breathing.'

'It is a shock no doubt,' he said, with compassion. 'To
come in alone, and hear such dreadful news! Don't
disturb her, Betty. I shall be here all night, watching; if
she wakes, or rings for me, you will find me here.'

Betty curtseyed and went away. Marcus returned to
the bedside and took his place beside it. The nurse built
up the fire, and settled herself on a chair close by. Silence
fell on the two watchers, and the only sounds were the

crackle of the fire and the faint shallow breaths that Constance drew.

The long hours of vigil passed. The fire burned low, and was replenished. Still Marcus sat, unmoving, his sister's hand clasped in his own; his eyes fixed on her still face.

And at last, as the first rays of dawn lightened in the east, and the night wind that sighed across the moors and rippled the lake died into silence, in the hush and stillness that is the precursor of a new day, Constance stirred.

His heart leaped as the slight fingers trembled in his own. Her eyelids fluttered, her eyes opened, and she looked at him, at the beloved face that hovered over her so anxiously; her mouth moved, and a thread of sound came from between her lips.

'Marcus,' she sighed, 'so thirsty—may I have a drink?'

A glad cry rose in his throat and came out as a husky whisper.

'Connie! Connie!' he said. 'Thank God! You're going to be all right!'

'Yes—' she said drowsily. 'But just now—so tired.'

The nurse brought the saline draught. He lifted her gently and held the cup to her mouth. She drank thirstily; gave him a fleeting smile; and sank back on the pillows, instantly falling into a deep and healing sleep. He touched her forehead; it was cool; her breathing deep and regular; her body relaxed. A faint natural colour tinged her cheeks.

Marcus got up and went to the window, pulling the curtains back. He looked out over the treetops, but scarcely saw them, for his eyes were filled with tears of thankfulness. He pictured Bethesda's joy and relief when she knew the outcome. He would kiss her awake with the happy news, and together they would compose a letter to Lady Cumnor, to tell her that Constance had met with an accident; but—she was recovering. The ending might have been so different! His mother would travel post-haste, of course, to Connie's bedside, to nurse her daughter back to health. But what could have been a family tragedy, darkening all their lives, would after all end happily.

His lordship looked at his watch. It was a few minutes before six o'clock. There was time for him to rest for an hour, be shaved and dressed. Then he would awaken Bethesda.

CHAPTER
EIGHT

As six o'clock struck on that grey damp morning, Bethesda was fitfully dozing in one corner of the ponderous green-and-gold Accommodation coach as it swayed and rocked on its way to Liverpool. Fortune had favoured her escape in every way. Hurrying across the fields until she struck the road, she had set out to cover the seven miles to the nearest town on foot, hoping to find an obscure lodging there in which to hide, while darkness still held. She knew that as soon as her absence was discovered, Marcus would scour the countryside. She considered hiring a post-chaise and making for London, but dismissed the idea. Marcus kept his teams stabled at every posting-house on the Great North Road, and would soon overtake her. But if she could reach the town, and obtain a seat on the mail coach to Liverpool, she could lodge in the poorer part of the city, and thus elude him. Beyond that, her thoughts did not go. She had no plans for the future; nor did she care.

Plodding along the dark road in the drizzling rain, eyes fixed blankly before her, she scarcely heard the sound of approaching hooves; until a sturdy gig, going past, was checked, and waited for her to draw level. Poised to take flight, she dimly made out a round beaming face atop a stout form behind the ribbons. A broad country voice called to her.

'Art going far, lass? 'Tis very wet, and lonely too, for a lass walking alone. Where are you bound for?'

Bethesda summoned her dazed wits and informed him in faltering tones that she was making her way to Liverpool, to seek a situation there. If she could reach the town, she could buy a ticket on the mail coach. She thanked heaven for the close bonnet that shadowed her face. It was a Ribston man who addressed her, and if he should recognise her, then the game was up.

But the possibility of coming upon the Viscount's cherished bride, walking unattended along a dark muddy road at night, did not even remotely cross the farmer's mind. He took her for a superior servant, lady's maid perhaps, and said in kindly tones,

'Well jump up lass, and come with us to the town. You are in luck. The mail leaves King's Arms at ten o'clock.' He stretched a hand to help her, and added consolingly, 'Lost your place, have you? Never mind. There's plenty of work for a smart lass in the big houses. Move over, Martha, and give the girl room. Now come up, Bess,' and the gig moved off. Wedged between his solid form and the well-cushioned figure of his comfortable wife, Bethesda was carried at a brisk pace into the outskirts of the town. He and his rib, the good man informed her cheerfully, had been visiting their married daughter, and were now on their way home. They would pass close enough to the King's Arms for her to walk to the inn. From there, she could board the stagecoach.

All fell out as planned. The yawning clerk at the booking office, rubbing his sleepy eyes, hardly looked at her as she paid for her ticket on the stage. The great coach came lumbering into the inn yard; with bent head she climbed aboard and shrank into a corner seat. As soon as the steaming horses had been replaced by a fresh team, the huge vehicle moved off, with a lurch and a heave, into the night.

In after years she could never recall very much of that journey. She was sometimes aware of times when the coach stopped to set down or take up a passenger, or for a pike keeper to open a gate along the road. But mostly she sat staring blankly at the darkness outside the window, oblivious to the rocking discomfort and the cold airs that crept in around the passengers' feet. Successive waves of misery and despair washed over her. Time and again she fought back the hot desperate tears. She must not think, must not, would not. He was lost to her, for she had brought tragedy and pain upon him and his family. She would never see him again. But to leave him thus—! A tearing sob rose in her throat and was forced back. It had to be; there was no other way; he must forget her. The death of Constance would lie always between them, a shadow, a curse upon their love. He must divorce her. It was easy enough to be legally free of a runaway wife. He would soon be able to marry again— as he must, for he was the heir, and it was his duty. And she knew that every night for the rest of her days, as she drifted into sleep, she would see his face, run towards him, and be gathered into his arms.

Deposited at length in the bushy courtyard of the large hostelry that served as terminus for the mail, Bethesda stood alone. Bandbox at her feet, ignored by the hurrying ostlers and baggage boys who passed to and fro. It was bitingly cold. She looked rather wistfully at the brightly lit entrance to the inn, where some other passengers were entering the welcoming portals. But this place would not do; Marcus would soon find her here;

she must seek quieter, more obscure lodgings. This inn
was too public, too well-known. She could not remember when she had last eaten anything, but she felt no
hunger; only a faint singing in her ears. Another lady, a
comfortable body in a poke bonnet and paisley shawl,
had just alighted from the stage; encouraged by her
motherly aspect, Bethesda ventured to ask, in a low
voice, could the lady direct her to some other lodging-
house, respectable, but less expensive?

After a brief consultation with her rubicund husband,
who was standing beside her, the kindly woman replied
that perhaps the Pelican Inn, in Ruthven Lane, might be
more suited to miss's requirements. With a soft word of
thanks, Bethesda picked up her bandbox. The world
tilted for a moment as she bent and straightened up
again. She closed her eyes, and steadied herself; and set
off along the footpath. Without much difficulty, she
found the Pelican, engaged a bedchamber, and presently entered a low-ceilinged coffee room, with one long
table, and leadlight casements covered by wooden shutters. The room was unoccupied. A satisfactory fire
burned in an old-fashioned hearth, on either side of
which wide oak settles had been built. Bethesda's knees
were shaking. The singing in her ears grew louder; she
sank gratefully down upon the wooden seat, and her
head came in sudden contact with the high uncushioned
back. The next minute, she had slumped sideways, as
misty blackness swam over her senses.

She opened her eyes to find a concerned face bending
over her. It belonged to a plump young woman of some
twenty summers, soberly and decently clad, in a dark
grey bonnet and pelisse. She had a round fresh face, a
resolute chin, and rather fine brown eyes, which were
fixed on Bethesda with an anxious look.

'Are you unwell, miss?' she asked, in a brisk West Country voice. 'Joshua and me found you a-fainting, when we came in just now. Are you staying in the Inn? Have you been ill?'

'No, I thank you,' Bethesda replied faintly, struggling up on one elbow. 'I am not ill, just very tired; and—I think—in want of some food.'

'Well,' replied the young woman cheerfully, with a broad smile that revealed an attractive set of dimples in her plump cheeks, 'that's easy to remedy! Josh and I are sharp-set too, I can tell you, after travelling all night! Ring the bell, and bespeak breakfast!'

'New South Wales!' cried Bethesda. 'New South Wales! You cannot be serious!'

Thunderstruck, she stared open-mouthed at her new-found friends. The remains of breakfast, of which husband and wife had partaken heartily, had been cleared away. Bethesda had not been able to swallow very much; a lump in her throat kept rising to choke her, and the eggs and ham which Mary and Joshua Hoby had attacked so heartily had seemed tasteless in her mouth. However, a mugful of hot coffee had restored her somewhat, and a faint touch of colour had returned to lighten the pallor of her face.

Now, elbows on table, chin on hands, she sat in stunned surprise, facing the young married pair seated across the table. Their kindly concern had supported her through the meal; a little food had put fresh strength in her; her spirits had lifted just slightly, under the bracing influence of Mary's cheery common-sense. She had proffered her story—she was a governess who had lost her place, and had come to seek a situation in Liverpool

—and they had accepted it without question. In return for this confidence, Mary had smilingly informed her that she and Joshua, her man, were bound that very day for the distant colony of New South Wales.

'New South Wales!' she exclaimed again, wide-eyed in amazement. 'Surely you do not mean it! Why, that is a penal colony!'

'It's a lot more than that, miss,' answered Mary roundly. 'It's a place where the likes of Josh and me can own land. There's convicts there, that's true. But there's free settlers, like us, going there as well. And that's where us two'—she reached for her husband's hand—'are bound for. We're off to a new life, miss; and it's all settled. We board the ship at noon!'

'To-day?' said Bethesda. 'So soon? It scarce seems possible! And surely' she paused, as a faint memory of lessons at the globe, far away at Miss Skeffington's, came to her mind, 'surely, New South Wales is a very great distance from here?'

'One hundred days, in a fast schooner,' explained Joshua. 'The convict ships are slower, of course. But Cap'n Percy's *Albatross* is moored this minute, out in the main channel; and we board her at noon; and sail on the afternoon tide.'

'But—but why?' demanded Bethesda. 'Why are you leaving England? So far—so long a journey! You may never come back again!'

'No, miss, we might never,' answered the young husband stoutly. 'We've made up our minds to that. You see,' he continued, in his broad West Country voice, 'I'm but the youngest son, out of four; and though our farm's a good one, there's no land for me. And in New South Wales there's a place—here, Mary, give us a hand—'

and he produced from his pocket a rolled-up map. This was spread out on the table, and the three heads bent over it, following the direction of his thick forefinger. 'See, miss, out beyond these mountains—they call 'em Blue Mountains—there's great wide plains, with good grazing for flocks. And a man like me can take up land there. I've got a letter—' he took it from another pocket —'from my cousin Jacob, who's been there four years; and he's mighty pleased with his wool clip, which he just sold in Sydney Town; and that's good enough for me. Here, miss, read for yourself.'

'And we've scrimped and saved, and we've got the ship's fare, and something over, to set ourselves up,' added Mary. 'And we're off, and no looking back.'

'We're cabin passengers, too,' said Joshua proudly. 'My Mary's not going to travel steerage, never you mind!'

There was a long silence in the room. The only sounds were the falling of an ember on the hearth; the ticking of the clock; and the whispered conversation of the young couple opposite her, who were perusing the map once again, and examining, for the fiftieth time, the contents of the letter. Bethesda sat rigid, her gaze going past them, seeing another face, blue eyes looking into hers; strong hands that reached to clasp her own. She swallowed, and reached into the depths of her cloak, fingering her purse. It was fairly well filled; she had drawn a hundred pounds from her banker's before journeying north to Yorkshire. Almost all that sum remained. She lifted her chin, and set her jaw firmly. Then she heard her own voice, rather husky, speak into the silence of the room.

'The *Albatross*, I think you said? Is she full—are all

the cabins taken? And if not—then tell me, if you please, where may I book a passage to New South Wales?'

Lord Mainwaring sat at the carved mahogany desk in his panelled study and stared moodily before him. The wide fireplace was swept clean, and a brass screen stood before it. The low casements were open, and a soft cool breeze stirred the curtains. Outside in the sunlight, the brief summer flowers bloomed on the moors, while above the pale waters of the mere flights of birds glided and dipped; the reeds at its edge showed white tips of blossom.

Marcus shoved aside the litter of papers on his desk, got up restlessly and went to the window. He twitched the curtains and let them fall. Three months! Three months, and it might be hours, so deep was the hurt, the loss, the physical pain of her absence. Three months of endless searching, all fruitless. A small army of his agents had combed the length and breadth of England. She was not to be found. It was as though, on the night when she had walked out of his house, she had walked out of the known world. A vision of her being set upon in some malodorous alley, her body thrown into the Thames, haunted his dreams. His nights were misery, picturing her alone, in sorrow, in danger. When he slept, it was but fitfully, for her face haunted his dreams, and he would start into wakefulness, her name upon his lips. He sighed, left the window, and returned to the cluttered desk; the reports from his agents were there; perhaps there might be something—some point he had overlooked—

The door opened, and Constance entered. She trod softly to where he stood, head bent, frowning over the closely written sheets. She laid her hand on his arm, and said,

'Is there no fresh news, love?'

'None,' he answered briefly. There was a silence. Then he turned to her and said hoarsely,

'Connie, I'm afraid. It's too long. I am beginning to fear that she—that she might be—'

'No, no!' his sister cried out. 'Don't say so! I won't believe it—I know she is alive—I am sure of it!' She threw her arms about his waist in a passion of love and sympathy. 'She will come back to us, Marcus—I know she will!'

'I will try to believe it,' he said heavily, 'because if she don't, then I can't tell how I shall go on without her, for the rest of my days.'

She buried her face in his chest and hugged him close. Unnoted by either of them, the study door had opened, and a deferential cough was heard close by. As they drew apart, the butler said,

'Forgive me, my lord, I was reluctant to disturb you; but there is a person without, who insists on speaking with your lordship. He came to the back door, my lord, and in the ordinary way, would never have been admitted. But under the circumstances I thought it best to inform you. The man says he has something to say, and will speak to none but yourself, my lord.'

'Who is he?' demanded Marcus. His brows snapped together.

'He refused to give his name, my lord; a very rough uncouth person, if I may say so.'

'Send him in!' ordered his lordship. 'Quickly, man! Don't you see—he may know something!'

The butler bowed, and returned in a few minutes,

ushering in a burly individual, of some forty years of age. The man's eyes shifted nervously in his sockets, and he clutched a battered cap in none-too-clean hands. His heavy boots were mud-caked and an unmistakable aura of the stables hung about him. When he spoke, his voice was rough and hoarse. Casting a lowering glance at the butler, he said, with blustering truculence,

'I've come to do you a good turn, your lordship. But I ain't speaking at all unless I see you in private.'

'You had better speak, my friend, and without delay,' said the Viscount unpleasantly. 'Out with it, man. What is it that you know?'

'What's in it for me?' demanded the groom, for such he plainly was.

The next moment he was lifted half off his feet, as two iron hands fastened on his throat, and shook him violently. His bulging eyes looked into the Viscount's, and before the concentrated fury of that blue glare, he wilted visibly. The blazing eyes seemed to spear into his brain, and a stream of words fell croaking from his mouth.

'I knowed it was her—I seen her face—though I only saw her the once—the night he took her from the big house; but—but she ain't the sort that you could forget—' his voice died away into a strangled gasp.

The Viscount released his grip. 'Go on, or it will be the worse for you,' he said with deadly quiet.

'Standing on the wharf she was, with the others,' stammered the groom. 'I watched when she was rowed out to the ship. It was her, no mistake, my lord, as God's my judge! I seen her face, and I remembered her! S'elp me, my lord! It weren't my fault, none of it, I swear! He made me do it!'

Marcus stood rigid, staring at the man. Barrington's henchman! Eyes slitted, nostrils white, he stood, while Constance gripped her hands together, and held her breath.

'A ship!' the Viscount shouted. 'She took ship! When? Curse you, you scum—when? Answer me or I'll kill you! What ship? And where was it bound?''

Lady Cumnor looked at the two young people standing side by side before her and, for the first time in her life, felt utterly and completely taken aback.

'You—you have taken my breath away,' she stammered. 'I don't know what to say. Constance—my dearest child! You cannot possibly be serious! I could never, never consent to such a thing!'

'Mama, we must,' said her daughter.

'But—so long a journey! So many months away! It does not bear thinking of! I cannot—I can't—' she stopped; her voice died helplessly away; she sat in distress, gazing at the two faces that looked so pleadingly back at her.

'I cannot let Marcus go alone, Mama,' Constance said firmly. 'We must go together. We shall take care of each other. Please, dearest Mama; please say yes; I have set my heart on it.'

'But the discomforts!' her mother moaned. 'The hazards of such a voyage! And so soon after your illness—it is unheard of!'

'I am quite well now, Mama,' Constance pointed out. 'The sea air will do me good, I expect.'

'The ship is fast, and comfortable, ma'am,' the Viscount chimed in. 'The *Southern Cross*, under Captain Pierce. She is a wool clipper, returning to Sydney Town with passengers and goods. She lies at Plymouth, and sails on Monday next.'

'Monday!' cried the stricken Countess. 'Dear God! I cannot take it in! Monday! I must be in a nightmare!'

The brother and sister stepped forward and laid their arms around the afflicted lady's shoulders.

'Dearest Mama,' said Constance gently, 'we must find Bethy and bring her back. Barrington's groom actually saw her embark on the *Albatross*. All our friends are praying that Marcus will find her. Everyone is waiting to welcome her back. The whole town is saying what a shocking thing that Barrington's jealousy should cause him to commit such a crime; and that it is lucky he went over the cliff by accident. No-one knows the full story, nor ever will. You know Martin can be trusted; he is part of the family. It is only natural that she should run away, thinking as she does that I am dead, and blaming herself for it. But we must find her, Mama! We cannot rest until she is found!'

'But what of Barrington's groom?' faltered the Countess. 'He knows the whole, from the very beginning; about the meeting at the school, and the abduction, and Marcus's·rescue in the nick of time. How is his mouth to be stopped?'

'Quite simply,' answered the Viscount. 'We are taking him with us to the colonies. He deserves to be hanged, of course; but with a good sum of money in his fist, and his fare paid, he can set up as a landowner in New South Wales; his silence is assured, in return for such a chance! I only wish—' he clenched his fists—'that he had spoken to me sooner. Three months! I could kill him for that!'

Constance slipped her hand through his arm.

'He was afraid, love,' she pointed out gently. 'He

feared that you would have him thrown into Newgate. Only for the fact that he could not find employment, after his master's death, and was desperate, he might never have spoken at all.'

'I should like very much to see him in Newgate, or preferably drawn and quartered,' growled the Viscount. 'As it is, he will doubtless become a prosperous settler in New South Wales, and lead a life of blameless respectability, surrounded by a deferential family, and highly regarded by his descendants!'

'I should think it very probable,' agreed Constance, 'and surely, in the circumstances, that is the best way. He will be satisfactorily established, and must keep silent, because if he ever speaks, he will have everything to lose. But, Mama! Please tell us! What is your answer?'

'Heaven help me!' responded her mother. 'I can see you mean to have your way—both of you. We had best lay this scheme before your father, without delay. What he will say, I shudder to think!'

'He will agree, if you give your consent, Mama,' said Constance firmly; and, after a lengthy discussion with the stunned Earl, so it proved; and the necessary prepartions for the long journey were set swiftly in motion. There was no time to be lost; the schooner was due to weigh anchor in less than a week; but fortunately, there were minions in plenty to attend to all the necessary details, and all was in readiness for the departure of the Viscount and his sister on the appointed day.

CHAPTER
NINE

Mr David Aubyn, master of Bellethorpe, settled his wide-brimmed hat firmly on his short black curls and stepped briskly towards the circular quay. Around him bustled all the noise and excitement of the arrival of a ship at the wharf in Sydney Town. Every citizen in the colony was there, it seemed, in the hopes of receiving goods ordered months ago, or long-awaited letters and journals from home. These last were being distributed to a waiting group standing around the mail sacks, which had been opened, and their contents tipped out on the ground. As the names on the letters were called, the lucky recipient stepped forward to claim his mail; those who waited in vain, until the last name was shouted, went sadly away, with heavy hearts. There were other excitements to amuse the spectators. Household goods, farm implements, wooden chests bound with rope, were unloaded from the hold and stacked upon the wharf. There was even a pianoforte, swathed in heavy cloth, which was lowered carefully to the ground. It was destined to travel by bullock dray to a remote property on the western plains, where a sun-dried lady with roughened hands had long been awaiting it. There, where the pure crisp winds swept keenly across the vast empty grasslands, would be heard once more, in a low split-shingle homestead with spreading verandahs, the songs of home which had once so pleased her husband, and would soon charm his ears again, in the lamplit evenings. There were pleasures in store for the ladies of the colony, too, when those intriguing wooden chests should be unpacked, and the contents revealed. The day of the gold rushes had not yet dawned. Wool was king, prices were high, and the sheep men were prospering. A surprising number of elegant gowns, bonnets, shawls and tippets, straight from the London modistes, were contained in those boxes, to be exclaimed over and tried on in high-ceilinged bedrooms that led onto cool verandahs. Those settlers who had capital to establish themselves lived in dashing style, and their ladies, though suntanned and lined by English standards—for they worked beside their men, most of them, and even rode at the mustering—were still able to indulge themselves in stylish dress; appearing at balls and parties in full evening splendour; dancing the night through, and making light of a journey of fifty miles to attend a race-meeting or ball. Convict labour was free to the settlers, but it was still necessary for the wife of a pastoralist to turn her hand to all manner of things that would never have been expected of a gentlewoman in England. Yet they had style, these colonial matrons, though not many could match the grandeur of the formidable Mrs Beaulieu, doyen of them all, whose carriage was flanked by forty outriders in full livery, whenever she chose to drive in from her husband's sprawling property beyond Camden Town.

Amid piles of heaped-up baggage the ship's passengers had disembarked, and now stood in little groups, gazing around in a bewildered way at the rough strangeness of the place. A sharp wind blew off the harbour, and a sun of incredible brilliance beat down on the scene. Its rays, reflected from the myriad dancing wavelets of the bright waters, cast moving reflections that dazzled un-accustomed eyes.

David Aubyn moved towards the passengers, scan-ning the faces of the various new arrivals. He had been commissioned by his friend Jacob Hoby to meet Jacob's cousin and his wife, and to convey them to Redmond, the Hoby property that adjoined his own. A rattling good fellow, Jacob, the best of good friends; impossible to find a better neighbour. David was, he assured Jake, only to happy to oblige him. It would suit him well, in fact, to spend a few days in Sydney Town, on business. Jacob need have no fears; Joshua and Mary would receive a warm welcome.

'For I dursn't leave the lass, you see,' explained Jacob, his honest face shining with mixed pride and anxiety. 'Her time's so close; could be any day; and she wants me here, do y'see, lad.'

'Of course she does,' David replied, 'And it's my pleasure to meet your cousins, I assure you. When I return I expect to greet you, Jake, as the father of a fine bouncing boy.'

'Aye, I do hope so,' said the expectant father, with a rueful grin, 'this waiting do wear a man down, to be sure. Nay, you wait, lad, until its your turn!'

'Give me time,' said David grinning, 'and present my best regards to Mistress Meg, if you please!'

Searching now for a set of features that resembled Jacob's, David was oblivious of certain admiring glances cast his way by the various local damsels who knew him by sight. His property, Bellethorpe, encompassed thous-ands of acres of rolling pastures, out beyond Bathurst, the new raw western town that was mushrooming as a local centre for the vast holdings that were being taken up on those endless western plains. Setting aside his wealth, however, David was himself sufficient reason for catching a lady's attention. He was twenty-nine years old, and of slightly above medium height, but appeared less because of the breadth of his shoulders. He was correctly and pleasingly dressed in a well-tailored riding coat and neat buckskins, which clung to his sturdy thighs. His tanned face was lit by a flash of white teeth; crisp black glossy curls clustered on his forehead; and a pair of honest brown eyes, frank and friendly, gave his whole countenance an engaging air that made instant appeal to members of both sexes alike. He was universally liked in the colony, though some among the other pastoralists complained that he was too easy with his convict labourers. Bellethorpe boasted no whipping-post. The cat o' nine tails was forbidden on Aubyn property. How the devil, grumbled the gentlemen over their wine, could one keep these miserable felons in their place, when Aubyn pampered them, housed them like free men, doubled their rations, and even paid them wages for good work? To these criticisms David replied that he had little trouble with absconding convicts; nor did he have much difficulty in keeping these 'double-distilled villains' (as Governor Darling had described them) productively at work. Jacob Hoby, his friend, was just such another, with these unheard-of ideas; and the diehards, shaking their heads, and prophesying ruin for both of them, could not deny that Bellethorpe and Redmond were prospering. Jacob, after only four years at Redmond, could already afford to build a very good homestead for his Meg. In spite of his outlandish ideas, however, it was generally agreed that Aubyn was the best of good fellows; and if one overlooked his eccentric behaviour in regard to his convicts, nobody could find a man more respected in the colony, which, since the great plains beyond the coastal ranges had become accessible in 1813, had swelled in numbers to almost a hundred thousand souls.

David's attention was suddenly arrested by a group of three people, standing a little apart from the crowd, looking around in some anxiety, surrounded by boxes and trunks. He quickened his stride; there could be no mistake; the resemblance between Jacob and his cousin Joshua was very marked. They could almost have been brothers. Hand outstretched, warm words of welcome on his lips. David stepped forward smiling.

A little flurry of excited greetings and explanations followed. Mary Hoby caught Bethesda's hand, and drew her forward. 'This is Miss Carfax, who travelled with us,' she informed David. 'She is a governess, Mr Aubyn, and hopes to find employment in the colony.'

David smiled into Bethesda's eyes. 'Welcome, Miss Carfax, to New South Wales,' he said warmly. Bethesda felt her hand taken in a firm friendly grasp; frank brown eyes smiled into her own; and in that instant a true and abiding friendship was born between them. She sensed immediately that here was a man to be trusted, relied on, a man of strong convictions, rocklike and unchanging; a man as clean and unsullied as the dancing sunlight that bathed them all, as they stood there on the wharf.

'Let me get you all settled at the inn,' David said. 'You must be in need of rest. To-morrow, I will take you to the Lands Office, Joshua; a few days are needed to complete formalities for your holding; and then we may all make for home, where your cousin is awaiting your safe arrival. He is most anxious to see you both.'

'Aye, and we are to see him,' agreed Joshua heartily. 'Lead on to tavern, lad. Happen Mary have not got her landlegs back yet, and truth to tell, the ground is rocking under my own pins, as though I were standing on a horse's back!'

Some five days later, seated in David's comfortable carriage behind a matched team that Marcus would not have despised, Bethesda and the Hobys set out towards Parramatta, along the good macadamised road laid down by the fore-thinking Governor Macquarie. Gangs of convicts in leg-chains were to be seen, working along the road; each in charge of a burly overseer, broad-hatted, lash in hand. Bethesda turned her eyes away, and met David's brown ones, looking at her a little anxiously.

'It's a rough new place, and such sights are distressing, I know,' he said. 'I own, I look forward to the day when the penal system is altered, and no more convicts are sent to these shores. But one must recollect—such things occur in England, too; only they are hidden from our view, unless we venture into the prisons. And in extenuation, I must point out that these felons, at least, have some chance for the future. When freed on a ticket-of-leave, they can start a new life. When you attend the Governor's dress balls, you will meet, even perhaps dance with, ex-convicts who are now men of substance in the colony.'

'Aye, Beth, the lad is right,' Joshua broke in. 'They have a better chance here, and live cleaner too, than those who are rotting alive in the hulks on the Thames.'

She was silenced; and indeed, the good sense of his words could not help but appeal to her. 'Do you use convicts to work your estate, Mr Aubyn?' she asked, after a short pause.

'I do,' he answered. 'I must, for there is, at present, no other source of labour. But when you see Bellethorpe, Miss Carfax, I believe you will not totally condemn the practice.'

The party spent a reasonably restful night at the Emu Ferry Inn, on the banks of the lovely Nepean River. They were ferried across on the following morning, and began ascending into the sandstone plateau. They passed through the deep cutting of Mount Victoria, and from thence approached the bare limitless plains of the west. Here, the road petered into a rough track; and though Bethesda was accustomed to the rugged outcrops and windswept moors of Yorkshire, she had never imagined distance so endless, a sun so merciless, or silence so profound. It was as though they had travelled off the edge of the known world, and entered another, primeval, strange, and almost fearful in its emptiness. The vast sky arched away above them, and as the day advanced, and the sun climbed, the brown earth began to give off waves of heat, even though here at the ends of the earth it was the winter season. Bethesda tried to imagine what the summertime must be like, here in this unbelievable place; and failed. Surely, she thought, no human being could spend his life here, and be happy.

Not that it mattered. She would never know happiness again.

David, watching her profile, as she looked from the carriage window, noted the tightening of her lips and the furtive wiping away of a tear with one gloved hand. He was aware of her extraordinary beauty, as any man must be; and being naturally perceptive, he had noticed during the past days that she was not happy. At first he had put it down to homesickness, and bewilderment, in what must seem to her an appalling place. But he now sensed that it was something more than that. Further, he did not think that she was, nor ever had been, employed as a governess. She was so obviously an aristocrat; every word and gesture, the proud lift of her chin, the imperious flash of her wonderful eyes, bespoke the lady of quality, accustomed to move in the first circles from babyhood. He was convinced that there was some mystery attached to her. A young girl—she could not be more than eighteen, if that—obviously of gentle birth, to voyage alone to New South Wales! It was unheard of. He thanked heaven that she had been fortunate enough to fall in with the Hobys, and to travel under their protection; and at least, she would be safe enough at Bellethorpe, until he could win her confidence, and discover what trouble or tragedy was shadowing those brilliant eyes, and drooping the corners of that lovely and wilful mouth.

'I count myself fortunate to have met you, Miss Carfax,' he said now. 'For some time I have been hoping to set up a school on Bellethorpe. There are some half-dozen children on the station, and my mother, before she died, had already ordered the erection of a suitable building for a schoolhouse. She felt strongly that the children of the colony ought to have the chance of education; and I agree. I am pleased to have found—' there was just the briefest pause—'a governess, actually in Sydney Town.'

She turned her head. 'I shall try to give satisfaction,

sir,' she said, in her best imitation of a deferential
servant's tones. A gleam of mischief twinkled in his eye,
and after a moment, she smiled fleetingly, as a glance of
understanding flashed between them. How clever he
was! He knew that she was pretending; but she was not
afraid; he would not give her away, and neither would he
pry into her secret. I could confide in Mr Aubyn, she
thought, and perhaps, one day, when I can bear to speak
of it . . . In the meantime, I shall try to be a good
governess.

They came to Bellethorpe in the late afternoon, after
a long and tiring day. The bullock dray laden with the
Hoby's boxes and household goods was well behind
them, for its progress was slow on the rough road, and
David's chaise had long outstripped it. The homestead
of Bellethorpe stood on a gentle rise, facing the sunrise,
looking across the spreading expanse of yellow-brown
grasses, rippling in the dry wind that blew monotonously
from the illimitable distance to the west. A fenced home
paddock surrounded the house, and a rough-hewn but
massive set of gates led them up a long avenue, which
somebody had planted with English trees. The house
was wide and low, with several chimneys; it was surrounded by a broad verandah, supported by solid heavy
posts over which climbing roses and wisteria vines
flourished.

The carriage drew up before a flat stone step; a man
ran from somewhere at the side of the house, to take the
horses' heads, shouting over his shoulder at some under-
ling away in the background. A bustle and stir and
barking of dogs broke out; the front door was swung
wide, and a stout comely woman in a calico gown and
white mob cap came surging forward, beaming, and

crying out to them, as the chaise door opened and the steps were let down.

'Master David!' she cried. 'Well, and I'm that glad to see you, lad! Heggarty has gone across the back paddock, already, to tell Master Hoby you'm back! And oh, Master David, such rejoicing at Redmond, sir, for Mistress Hoby do have a son—a fine boy, nine pounds on the storeroom scales—yesterday morning, it was, and both well, the Lord be praised!'

David jumped from the chaise, grabbed the lady round her ample waist, and heartily kissed her firm rosy face. Bethesda, amazed and amused by so informal a meeting between master and servant, was visited by a fleeting memory of the Cumnor's stately major domo welcoming his lordship to Ribston; and could not repress a tiny chuckle. David, hand extended to help the travellers from the carriage, was wreathed in smiles.

'Joshua, did you hear?' he called. 'Splendid news—a son for Jacob! Heggarty's gone for him now; you may expect to see him soon. It's only fifteen miles to Redmond.'

'Come away in, then,' said the housekeeper, bobbing a token curtsey to the ladies, 'you must all be sharp-set, and Cook said to tell you, Master David, that you may dine as early as you please.'

The whole party was then swept indoors. Bethesda was ushered down a long wide hall and shown into a square whitewashed bedchamber, small, but high-ceilinged, with shuttered doors opening onto the verandah beyond. A young serving-girl entered, with a can of hot water, and enquired in a pert yet friendly voice if miss needed anything else. On receiving a negative reply, she closed the bedroom door rather noisily, and Bethesda was left alone.

A profound silence fell. Bethesda became conscious of the endless spaces outside, and the emptiness that stretched in every direction. She felt very small and very alone. The inexorable vastness of the ocean across which she had journeyed, the months of voyaging that seemed until now to have passed almost in a dream, the incredible distance of both time and space that now separated her from England, from Marcus, suddenly took shape in her brain; pressed upon her senses; sent her mind spinning. Despair broke over her; her brain reeled; she collapsed into a wooden chair that stood beside the narrow bed. Her head fell forward on her arms, and she gave way to a wild fit of weeping; racking sobs that set her body shuddering and seemed to tear her apart. A passion of misery and pain took possession of her. It was unthinkable, unbelievable, unbearable that she should be here, in this awful place, here to stay, forever, with her heart breaking, and her soul crying for him, until she died!

The tumbled curls spread over the white bedspread; bonnet and reticule fell unheeded to the floor. When at last she grew calmer, she still remained, head pillowed on her arms, wet black lashes in fringes on her cheeks, down which the tears had made furrows in the travel dust of that long journey across the plains.

A knocking on the door did not arouse her. Only when Mary Hoby bent over her, shaking her shoulder none too gently, did she lift her drenched eyes to meet Mary's gaze. During the long sea voyage the two girls had become good friends. Bethesda had come to realise that Mary's astringent manner hid a warm heart, and although she had not confided her secret, she had admitted to her new friend that an unhappy love affair had caused her to leave England. To this, Mary had replied with blunt common-sense that there were still many pebbles on the beach.

'Now, lass this won't do!' said Mary sharply, regarding her friend with an accusing eye. 'Just look at you! You are a disgrace! Bedraggled as an alley cat!' She picked up Bethesda's scattered possessions, and smoothed the rumpled bedspread. 'Get up, girl, and pull yourself together! There's no place for weaklings and cry-babies here, I can tell you that!'

Stung by these severe words, Bethesda sat up abruptly, and blinked indignantly at her accuser.

'How dare you!' she began, in haughty tones. She stopped; sniffed; and a reluctant, watery smile spread over her face. 'Mary, you wretch!' she went on, with a husky laugh, 'How dare you call me a cry-baby; I won't have it! You shall not say so!'

'Don't cry then,' said her friend prosaically. 'Show some spirit! A hot bath is what you need, girl, and your dinner in bed. As soon as I have greeted Cousin Jacob, as is proper, it's just what I'm going to have myself. In the morning, everything will seem better; you just see, lass, if I'm not right.'

And right, to a certain extent, Mary was. The following morning dawned cloudless and clear; so dry and crisp was the air that Bethesda's curls crackled and clung to the comb as she stood before the bedroom mirror. Breakfast had been served by a neat-footed, sharp-featured serving-girl, the same who had showed the visitors to their rooms on arrival. The housekeeper, Mrs Clancy, and the station cook made up the rest of the domestic staff, with the assistance of a young handyman who doubled as boots, scullery-man, keeper of the vegetable garden, and general off-sider around the house. All the house servants, and the men who worked outside upon the property, either were, or had been, assigned convicts. The homestead itself was unexpectedly spacious, and boasted a cosy breakfast parlour in addition to quite a large and formal dining room. From the windows of the breakfast room, a pleasant garden could be seen, laid out in neat walks and flower-beds; and beyond a low wall stood the orchard, with apple and orange trees, some already budding into early blossom. Bethesda could also discern, in a sheltered corner, a small pretty rose-garden, with a rustic seat in the middle. She exclaimed with pleasure, and David, joining her at the window, said,

'My mother was a great gardener, Miss Carfax. The trees in the home paddock accompanied her as seedlings, on the voyage here from England. My uncle in Suffolk kept her supplied with others, in successive years. The fruit trees in the orchard came from his orangery, and have flourished, as you can see.'

'Is it very long, sir, since Mrs Aubyn died?' Bethesda asked diffidently, after a short pause.

'Two years,' he answered quietly. 'My father was carried off by a sudden fever, and she did not long survive him. The summers in this place were hard for her to bear.'

'I—I, too, have lost my parents,' she said, with quick sympathy. He took her hand, and patted it; they exchanged a warm mutual glance; they had liked each other by instinct, and were on the way to being firm friends.

'Your mother—' she ventured, after a minute. 'Did she—was she happy here?'

He turned to her and smiled.

'You will find it hard to comprehend, I know,' he answered, 'but my mother truly loved this place, and never would willingly have left it. She worked to build it, side by side with my father, over the years. It is my legacy from them both, to hold and to keep. I, too, will never leave Bellethorpe. It is mine.'

There was a moment's silence. Then—

'I can understand that,' she said in low tones. He gave her a sudden intent look; but said no more.

Some saddlehorses had been brought round from the stables, to take the newcomers on a tour of the homestead and its precincts. On David's advice, Bethesda had laid out most of her remaining sovereigns on a serviceable riding habit, during their days in Sydney. Some necessary personal items, and a couple of Bengal cotton gowns, had exhausted her slender purse. David had offered her an advance on the yearly salary of twenty pounds which had been agreed on, but she had declined; the vehemence of her refusal, and the hot colour which had flooded her creamy skin, had rather surprised him; and he had said nothing further. The truth was, she was feeling both nervous and a little guilty at passing herself off as a skilled governess; and had visions of being dismissed, if it should turn out that she could not manage the station children, or teach them to read and write.

However, she was not expected to begin her duties today; and, twisting herself to and fro to get a better view in the small looking glass, she was not too dissatisfied with her appearance. The riding dress, of course, could not compare in quality or line with those especially made for her in London. Nor, as she extended one foot rather ruefully, could these distinctly solid boots be called in the height of fashion. But the dark green cloth set off her vivid colouring, and there was a small green hat, with brim upturned behind over her bunched curls, that became her quite well. As she waited on the front step with David and the Hobys, she could not but be aware of an admiring gleam in Mr Aubyn's eye.

The gleam turned to interest as she was tossed into the saddle and the party moved off. He saw at once, as she gathered the reins with practised hand, and began coaxing the stolid brown station hack into showing its paces, that she was a skilled horsewoman; and more than ever he became certain in his mind that she was no humble governess, nor ever had been. As they set off down the avenue at a brisk trot, he remarked casually,

'You are a notable rider, Miss Carfax; you have startled old Jemima into quite a show of spriteliness; did you hunt at home?'

She saw the trap too late to avoid it. Her cheeks were in a glow; the frosty air had a refreshing nip; and the delight of being on horseback, after so many months at sea, had lifted her spirits.

Impulsively, she replied,

'Oh yes, indeed! I was used to ride Papa's hunters from my early childhood; and when the scent was running breasthigh at Ansteys—'

She stopped short. The colour drained from her face; her eyes, wide with alarm, flew to his; she gasped, and caught her breath.

He flashed her a sidelong look, his brown eyes very intent. There was a breathless pause. Then, deliberately, he smiled, and said in a courteous tone,

'I must find you a more worthy mount. Your duties as governess will give you ample leisure time. I must only ask that you will not ride alone about the property. There is always the chance of meeting an escaped felon, and they are dangerous, and would kill you for the sake of the horse.'

'I shall remember,' she answered in a stifled voice, head bent to hide her face. She had given herself away completely; but she was not sure if he had understood. It seemed as if he had not realised the significance of her hasty words; and as they rode on, and David continued to converse with easy good manners with the whole party, her fears receded, and she felt sure that he had not noticed her mistake.

But as they skirted the fence of the homestead paddock and struck out an easy canter into the open, David's brain was working, his thoughts whirling. Ansteys! He had caught the word, and he knew the name. As a lad of fourteen he had left England with his parents. His father had been a younger son, and the family estates entailed. Theirs was one of the first sheep properties beyond the Blue Mountains. Bellethorpe had been granted to them in 1814. But before coming to the colony, David had been schooled at Eton. And among his contemporaries at that seat of learning had been a certain James Carfax, an engaging chatterbox, who laughingly deplored the poverty of his branch of the family, who spoke of his infant cousin Beth Carfax, who would inherit vast wealth; when she grew old enough, James was used to declare, he meant to try for her himself. James had painted a graphic picture of the enormous fortune that this little girl would in due course inherit. There was no male heir, and the estates would pass to a younger brother—the story was coming back. But—in God's name—what had happened to her parents? Wait—! Her words of that very morning came back suddenly. She had said that she, too, had lost her parents. Then that must mean—that must mean—

In a blinding flash of insight that hit him like a blow, David Aubyn suddenly realised that here, cantering along beside him, in this distant colony, alone, masquerading as a humble governess, entirely unprotected except for chance acquaintances, was none other than Carfax's only surviving child; heiress to one of England's greatest fortunes; a high-born lady, sheltered and cossetted since birth, here, on Bellethorpe; there could be no mistake. Great God in Heaven!

David was by habit level-headed and cool; but the shock of this discovery almost made him reel in the saddle. Bethesda had drawn a little ahead, to hide her confusion. He sat stunned, staring at her straight back, and the flaming cascade rippling over her shoulder, catching every glint of the clear sunlight. She could not, he realised, be over eighteen years of age, if even that. Numb with the shock, he rode like an automaton for several minutes. His first reaction, as feeling returned, was a surge of rage against her relatives. What on earth could they be about—how the devil did she come to be here, in such circumstances! How carelessly they must have guarded her! Whatever her reasons for running away, whatever family quarrel had caused her to behave so rashly, their conduct was inexcusable; she was a child, an innocent baby. When he thought of some of the hands into which she might have fallen, his blood ran cold. It had taken only a very short association with her for him to realise that beneath her enchanting exterior she was as vulnerable as a child, as confiding as a kitten, and as trusting. The whole affair was scandalous!

Well; those grand relatives of hers must, of course, be speedily informed of her safety and her whereabouts. Heggarty should take a letter to the coast to-morrow, to be carried to England on the first ship that sailed. He would pen the missive as soon as they returned to the house. He promised himself the satisfaction of a few sharp remarks on the subject of her guardians' negligence. In the meantime, however, he decided that he must keep silent. To confront the young lady with his knowledge of her identity would be, he decided, unwise. If she had fallen out so seriously with her relatives as to do such a desperate thing as this, and when she realised that he meant to inform them of her whereabouts, she was quite capable of trying to leave Bellethorpe. He could not permit that, of course; but the thought of having to keep her forcibly in his custody for several months, until some representative of her family arrived in the colony to claim her, held no appeal for him whatever! No; she must not guess that he knew who she was.

He forced himself, therefore, to smile and talk easily and naturally as they rode on, and he pointed out objects of interest; the stone sun-dial that had come from his mother's girlhood home in England, to stand in a colonial garden, surrounded by orange trees. The clear winding creek, fringed with trees, that ran over flat pebbles and from which his mother had given the property its name. The cool water was flowing freely, under the shady banks; but in times of drought it would shrink to a string of stagnant waterholds, in the burning heat. Then the station would depend on its dams and wells, whose positions were marked by tall windmills turning in the sharp breeze. The new arrivals were surprised by the variety of outbuildings that enclosed a horseshoe shaped area at the back of the house. Coach house, stables, exercise paddock, blacksmith's, saddler's, slaughter-house, dairy, store sheds, and a giant shearing shed where, David informed them, many dances had been held the night through. The comfortable servants' quarters and the vast kitchen were built on to the back of the house, for security; Bethesda had the barest possible acquaintance with kitchens of any sort, but she was impressed by its size and scrubbed cleanliness, and the huge fireplace, built of home-made bricks and stone. To English eyes, the buildings were plain and the landscape devoid of beauty. Yet there was an air of solidity, of permanence, about the whole; and the sprawling home-stead, its verandahs sloping so low that from a distance they seemed almost to meet the earth, had a quality of strength and stability that she could not help but admire.

'We are almost self-supporting,' David explained. 'Meat, butter, vegetables are our own; so are almost all household needs, such as candles and soap. Even our working boots are made here, for I was lucky enough to be assigned a cobbler, a few years ago. He is married to Joan, my cook, and they have several children—some of whom will be your pupils, Miss Carfax. Clothes, of course, and elegancies such as glass, china and wines, must be bought on visits to Sydney Town. But by and large we manage well enough.'

'Sir, you must be very proud of your home,' Bethesda said impulsively.

'Indeed, I am,' he answered, with a flash of white teeth in his browned face. 'The homestead as you see it was not built at first. My mother lived in a small slab hut, in the early years, and worked side by side with my father. Clancy, our housekeeper, came with us on that first journey over the mountains; she was an assigned convict; she travelled with my mother in a bullock wagon, and became part of our family. Heggarty, too, my head stockman, has been with us from the outset; so have several of the other men.'

'So—in a way—you have founded a dynasty,' said Bethesda slowly, in a wondering tone.

There was a short silence. Then Mary asked,

'Some of the convicts stay on then, after they are freed?'

'Yes; some prefer to stay and make their home on the station; others take up selections of their own. Your gang of assigned men, Joshua, will arrive in a week or two. They are travelling west with half-a-dozen new men allotted to me. We must choose a site, and make a start, as soon as may be, on your own new home.'

'Aye, indeed,' Joshua assented eagerly. 'Mary and me can't wait to have our own house. We thought to visit Cousin Jacob at Redmond to-morrow; we must greet Meg and the little one; and Jake has promised to advise us on the best situation for building on. Will you accompany us, lad?'

'Yes, I mean to go with you,' responded David. 'And you, Miss Carfax: would you care to visit Redmond to-morrow?'

'I should like to, very much,' she answered. 'But should I not begin my duties as schoolmistress? I saw a group of children, playing behind the servants' quarters. I must begin to earn my salary, sir.'

With a twinkle in his eye, he answered,

'I think your duties can wait a few days. The school-house, unused since my mother's death, must be made ready; I will let you know, Miss Carfax, when I wish you to open your school.'

'Thank you,' Bethesda said, in some relief. 'I—I do love children, sir, and I am sure I can teach them to cipher, and to read, at least a little. Only—you understand—I am as yet a little strange—and unaccustomed to . . .' her voice tailed off, and she looked a good deal confused.

'I am sure you will manage perfectly,' he said in encouraging tones. 'In fact, you will doubtless enjoy the task, and you will be doing something that was dear to my mother's heart.'

'I will do my best,' she said, quite subdued. It was on the tip of his tongue to tell her that she need not, after all, undertake the work; he would find her some more congenial and easy employment. He realised that she was actually anticipating her work with some nervousness; the wryness of the situation struck him; a great lady, accustomed to command a myriad of well-trained minions from childhood, afraid of a few colonial children! But, he reflected, with a gleam of amusement, the children would certainly love her, and it would do her no harm to contribute something useful to the colony while she remained under his protection. In addition, it would keep her busy, and while she was busy, she would be easier to keep under his eye. For guard her he must, with the utmost care. No clue to her identity must be allowed to escape, for her presence in the colony if it were known, would cause a furore, and the resulting gossip would be damaging for her, and the last thing that her family would desire.

CHAPTER
TEN

As Heggarty rode towards Sydney Town, carrying in his waist pouch the letter which was to go by the first possible sail to England, Constance was standing, muffled in a thick hooded cloak, within the firm circle of Marcus's arm. They were watching a flock of Cape pigeons, flying overhead, above the reefed topsail of the *Southern Cross*. The schooner was bearing down fast into the high latitudes, six hundred miles south of the Cape of Good Hope; and so mighty were the westerly winds that howled unceasingly over the deep cold seas, that the masts carried but little sail. Even so, the ship was making a speed of over fifteen knots. A pair of albatrosses followed swiftly in her wake. Above and around the two passengers on the deck were many sounds; hissing, roaring, flapping and slapping sounds, as the steady monotonous drone of the howling wind continued, as it had done for past centuries uncounted, and would, it seemed, for ever. Brother and sister loved to be on deck, wrapped to the eyes against the knifing cold, and watch the great waves roll in the same direction as the ship, as she perched sometimes on the crest of a mountain of water; or cowered deep in the trough, as if momentarily she must be engulfed.

Marcus bent his head to hers. 'Are you afraid?' he shouted, against the howl of the wind.

'Never!' she called back. 'I never enjoyed anything so much!'

The wind caught her words and whipped them away, but the sparkle in her blue eyes gave him his answer.

'Little adventuress!' he said, and pinned her close to his side, as the ship surged forward, under the giant rolling swell; beating onwards, day and night, running endlessly before the westerlies, with two muscular helmsmen always at the wheel; their course set firm for Sydney Town.

In the shingle-roofed hut built for a schoolhouse on Bellethorpe, Bethesda stood and surveyed her new pupils. There were nine of them, ranging in age from five to twelve years. They sat quietly on the benches made by the station carpenter, and gave her back stare for stare. Some looked apprehensive; some wary; one or two proffered a tentative smile. All had been firmly admonished by Mr Aubyn, who had escorted Miss Carfax in person to take up her new duties. With clean faces and folded hands, they waited expectantly to see what Miss would do first. The only sounds were the creaking of the wooden shutters and the voices of birds in the tree beside the door.

Looking at them made her very aware of the incongruity of her situation. It seemed impossible that she, Bethesda, should be standing here in this rough hut, facing with a distinct nervous qualm a group of urchins born to convict servants, some of them out of wedlock; currency children, David called them, and perhaps the term was apt, for they were considered free citizens, of value to the colony; the future of this land would depend in part on the sort of adults that they became. She understood the reason for the late Mrs Aubyn's concern with their education. As she regarded them, she saw that they showed none of the servile deference that children in similar circumstances in England would have displayed; on the contrary, they were scrutinising her, level-eyed, just as closely as she was observing them. She noticed too that they were tall and sturdy, clear-eyed, sun-tanned; with an air of self-reliance, almost of defiance, that accorded oddly with their motley assortment of clothing and their bare horny feet.

Well, she was spirited herself, and proud; and respected it when she met it in others. She suddenly smiled warmly upon them all, and looking around, said in a fair imitation of her erstwhile preceptress in that far-off schoolroom at Miss Skeffington's,

'Good-morning, children.' A ragged chorus of replies sounded. 'You will all please to stand. We will have morning prayers; and then I am going to teach you to sing a song together.'

David, hovering the near vicinity some half-an-hour later, ready to intervene on behalf of the new teacher—for he was only too well acquainted with some of the more ingenious tricks perpetrated from time to time by certain of the imps who had been unwillingly rounded up for school—heard the sound of children's voices raised in unison. Bethesda's rich contralto rose, strong and true, and most of the children were singing like blackbirds. Some were rather at odds with the tune, but peering cautiously through the shutter, he saw that they were all engrossed, their eyes fixed on Bethesda's vivid face, as she beat time for the music. Hands were clapping, feet tapping.

She had them round her thumb already, he thought,

grinning. I might have known it! What a darling she really is! I would like very much to know just why she gave those high-nosed relatives the bird; damn them; they could not have valued her as they ought!

As he strode away towards the shearing sheds, he reflected that he could not remember having ever seen a girl more beautiful, more spirited, or with a sweeter disposition. Setting aside her fortune, she was in herself a prize such as any man would be proud to win. And puzzling a little at the waywardness of human nature, including his own, he wondered why he had not fallen in love with her.

For he admired her, he felt warm friendship towards her, but he was not in love with her. In fact, had he been fortunate enough to be blessed with a young sister, he would have wished her to be just such a girl as Beth Carfax. And until she returned to England—as, eventually, she surely must—he intended to stand in place of her older brother, and guard her, keep her safe, in all things.

Days slipped by, and merged into weeks. Time seemed to pass unnoticed, Bethesda sometimes thought, in this primeval place. The apple trees in the orchard were breaking into blossom, and already, the brilliant sun, beating down from its zenith, gave promise of the blazing heat to come. The first flies of summer, vanguard of an army, bumbled and droned about the windows. Bethesda was glad to don one of the calico gowns that she had procured in Sydney, and to put on the wide-brimmed straw hat that Mrs Clancy produced from the cool depths of the storeroom. As she trod the narrow path that led to the schoolhouse, a short distance from the main buildings, the dry heat of a ruthless north wind struck her in the face. She realised, rather sadly, that no English complexion would survive undamaged through many summers in this place, and reminded herself that, after all, it did not matter. She would grow old here, forgotten by the world; no-one would care when her looks faded. She shook herself mentally. There was no use in self-pity.

The path was bordered by tall shrubs, sufficiently thick to form a leafy screen on each side, adding some coolness and shadow as she walked. David had warned her to watch where she trod, lest a sleepy snake should be lying across the track. She was safe, he hastened to assure her, unless she actually placed a foot upon one of the reptiles; even then the stout leather boots she wore would probably protect her. At first she had followed the path each day with a secret shudder; but practice had bred confidence. She was now almost unconcerned, though she still kept wary eyes on the ground ahead of her.

A rustle in the greenery behind her suddenly startled her. She stopped, and turned her head; for a moment, she thought she discerned a movement, somewhere behind her shoulder. She stood in mid-step, half-turned, and listened. But there was nothing more. Hesitating, she remembered David's firm instructions—on no account was she to leave the path, or to wander about. People had been known to become lost in the bush, he explained, almost within sight of a house. He must know, at any given time, where she was. It was necessary for her safety. She had seen the sense of that, and had readily acquiesced. Now, after listening for a minute, and hearing nothing more, she gave a little shrug and set off again to the schoolhouse. There was nothing to fear—some small wild animal, doubtless. By the end of the morning, when her pupils were released from lessons for the day, she had forgotten the incident. When she recalled it later, it seemed to trivial to mention. So close to the house, almost within call of the kitchen door, what could there be to harm her?

In the cool of the evening, Heggarty, head stockman and the master's trusted friend, came to the edge of the homestead verandah, where David sat in shadow, looking out across the spread of savannah parkland that never failed to bring him peace and satisfaction after the day was finished. Seeing his stockman approach, he beckoned, and Heggarty stepped on to the low platform, and squatted on his heels. After a few minutes of companionable silence, the stockman spoke in a low voice.

'The new man, Levitt, is causing trouble again,' he said. 'Another fight in the barracks this night. I don't know the full rights of it, but young Rogers has got a bloody mouth and there's some damage done as well. I don't like the looks of it, sir. We'd better be rid of Levitt and his two cronies. There was no trouble until they came.'

'Rogers is a good lad,' David said thoughtfully. 'Not the sort to start trouble.'

'I reckon he was goaded into it, sir,' Heggarty replied. 'That Levitt's the one, and he ain't about to change. Vicious and mean, Master Davey; and past praying for. Treat him with kindness, he takes it for weakness. Any other master, he'd get a taste of the cat to teach him a lesson.'

'No, Bill, you know my orders in that respect,' David said. 'You don't cure a man of vice that way. You make him worse. But we'll get rid of Levitt and the other two, Bill, if you think it best. I trust your judgment; always have. They shall go back to Sydney with the next team that goes down.'

'I know I'm right, sir,' the stockman said. 'Sometimes you get one, that's so far gone, they get twisted in their mind, like. Nothin' we can do to change their ways. Levitt goes on the next wagon, then, and good riddance. I don't trust him, sir, not for one minute. He was missing from roll-call this morning; and though he turned up later, I don't like the slippery way he goes about, stirring things up, picking the others; I won't be easy until he's gone, and his two cronies with him.'

'The wagon will go through to Sydney in a few days,' David said. 'Just keep him in your eye until then, Bill.'

'You bet your life I will,' said Heggarty grimly. He rose, and stepped to the ground; his lean figure was soon lost to sight in the shadows of the garden.

It was several mornings later when David, entering the breakfast parlour, encountered Bethesda as she was preparing to leave for her school.

'I must be away for a few days, Miss Carfax,' he said. 'I am riding to the western boundary with some of the men; we are in process of constructing a new dam there. It is some twenty miles distant, and I shall be camping for a few nights at the site. But Clancy will be here, and the house servants, and several of the men. You will be quite safe.'

'Yes, of course,' Bethesda answered. 'I understand, and am not at all nervous.'

'Heggarty will be in charge, during my absence,' David said. 'I can leave him with a quiet mind. He is totally reliable; my right arm.' He did not add that were it not for her presence on the station his head stockman would have accompanied him, for there was much to be done at the site of the dam, and every man was needed. But, even though Levitt and his two satellites had duly been despatched on their way to Sydney the day before, under armed guard, he was keenly aware of the responsibility of her welfare. Heggarty must stay, and in addition, two other men would remain in the barracks, as well as Rogers, the young lad who cared for the garden and generally assisted in the running of the house. He could get on with his work with an easy mind.

He did not know, that as he spoke, both the guard and the driver of the wagon had lain dead, for many hours. Their bodies had been dragged off the track, behind low bushes, out of sight from the road. The wagon, rifled of its contents, was roughly concealed under piled-up branches; and the four bullocks, stripped of their harness, were heading across country towards the nearest water-hole.

'Whereabouts is the dam being built, sir?' Bethesda asked, from politeness rather than from any real interest.

'Come here; I will show you,' he replied, taking her arm, and guiding her to the verandah. 'If you wanted to find it, you would ride out there, in a straight line, past the two beeches, and at right angles to the blacksmith's. You would keep that course for some twenty miles. Then, you would strike the bank of a creek; turn right; and follow its course; and you would come to the camp.'

'I see,' she murmured, rather absently. Her attention was caught by the delicate colours of the rose-garden, just coming into bloom; and a pang of longing for a real English garden had pierced her heart with a sudden pain.

Within the hour, David and the men set off. The bustle of their departure died away; the house and its surroundings settled back into silence. Returning from the school at midday, Bethesda made her way to the house, where she partook of cold mutton and fruit, and drank a cup of tea, under Clancy's benign eye. The quiet afternoon wore on. As evening drew in, Bethesda and Clancy dined together, in the housekeeper's cosy sitting-room; and afterwards, Bethesda carried a branch of candles to the drawing-room, and played and sang a few simple tunes at the pianoforte which had belonged to David's mother. He had been pleased to discover that she could play the instrument, and had bade her use it whenever she chose. Some of the music that Mrs Aubyn had used was yellowing, and in need of repair. Bethesda made a silent promise to busy herself on the morrow in mending the old sheets and binding them afresh. Hidden away among the others, she found a song that Constance was used to sing, in her clear soprano. Sudden memory came flooding back. The three of them, Marcus, Constance and herself, had joined together in singing that very melody, in the panelled drawing-room at Ribston, during the happy evenings of that last ill-fated visit to Yorkshire. Constance—who was dead; Marcus—whom she would never see again.

Tears filled her eyes. She closed the pianoforte; put away the music. And after that, there seemed nothing more to do, except to go to bed.

Huddled in the seclusion of her narrow white bed, she took refuge in a fit of weeping. This had the immediate effect of easing her pain; and it was not very long before she sank into sleep, a damp handkerchief still clasped in one hand, her unbound hair streaming over the pillow.

A sudden sound, sharp and strange, jerked her back into wakefulness. She sat up, wide-eyed in the darkness. A shot—a cry—she could not be sure. Could not even tell if she had dreamed it. Keeping perfectly still, she listened, straining her ears; she could hear nothing. The night air had turned chilly, and her impulse was to snuggle back into the warm covers. Almost, she had become convinced that it had been a dream, when her ears caught a whisper of sound; there it was again! A faint shuffling noise, as of a cautious footstep on the flagstones of the hall—outside her very door!

She gave a tiny gasp; and then, moving like a shadow, she slid from the bed and glided across the floor to the tall shuttered doors that led out to the verandah. Her hands found the bolt in the dark. She drew it back; it was well oiled and made little noise. She slipped between the shutters, and pushed them together behind her, just as the convict Levitt came through the door of her room.

He held a candlestick in one dirty hand. Its flickering gleam lit up a dark heavy face and red slitted eyes. His loose mouth fell open, showing rotting stumps of teeth. His squat heavy body, enormously strong, cast a grotesque shadow on the wall. Fumes of rum mingled with his sour breath. As he stood swaying, thick legs planted wide, his malevolent gaze took in the room, and the empty bed. He stood glaring for a moment; then he cursed roughly, and lurched across the room and crashed the shutters wide. The verandah was empty. He thudded to its edge, and stood, holding the candle high, and peering into the garden, beyond the circle of light.

The house was bordered on this side by a wide sweep of lawn. A clear moon lit up the scene; a frosty dew already coated the grass; nothing stirred in the stillness.

His evil eyes turned this way and that, his head jutted forward, his thick tangled hair almost covering the pig's eyes that gleamed under his shaggy brows. Nothing moved. Nothing stirred. No fleeing form, no flash of movement, could be seen in the empty garden. He stood still, light held high, and listened.

Almost directly beneath his feet, Bethesda lay, in frozen stillness. She had flung herself flat on the earth, under the verandah's edge, among the scanty shield of low bushes and shrubs that grew in the narrow garden bed along the verandah's length. Hugging the ground, she wriggled under the leaves, among the roots, close to the soil; held her breath; and lay still.

She could hear his hoarse breathing above her. Had he looked straight down beneath his feet, he must have seen her; for the shrubs concealed her only partially, and her nightgown was white. But he was peering beyond, holding the candle above his head, trying to see past the circle of light. She tried not to breathe; she was sure he would hear the frantic thumping of her heart. The night air was cold, and her body shook from head to toe in chill and terror. She hugged the earth and waited for the moment of discovery.

It did not come. He stood there, motionless, for perhaps a minute. Then he uttered an obscenity; the circle of light wavered; growling, he turned, and stamped away along the verandah towards the front of the house. His boots thudded on the boards. She heard him muttering, as he retreated, the light still held above his head, towards the corner of the house.

The moment he disappeared around the front, Bethesda rolled clear of the bushes and fled in the opposite direction. She flew across the lawn, expecting every moment to hear a shout behind her; and dived headlong for the blackness behind the stables. As she gained it, her foot caught; and in mid-flight she tripped and sprawled flat across the legs of a figure that lay stretched out in the grass, under the branches of the elm tree which shaded the blacksmith's shop on summer afternoons.

She hit the ground with a thud, and for a moment lay stunned, too shocked to utter the shriek that rose in her throat. Then as she scrambled to her knees, ready to run wildly into the night, away from the horrifying menace that was stalking her, a faint whisper, a thread of a voice, reached her ears.

'Miss!' it sighed. 'Miss—Miss Carfax!'

She turned, poised for flight, and in the diffused light made out the white anguished face and one hand half-outstretched in appeal. It was Rogers, the young convict who worked in the homestead garden. A thin lad, no older than herself, she knew him by sight, although she had never spoken to him. She saw with horror a dark stain spreading across his breast. Even in the dim light, the widening stain glistened. She reached out and touched it; it was blood. She fell on her knees beside him.

'Miss—get away!' the boy croaked. 'Levitt—looking for you—been watching you—you must get away . . .'

'But—what has happened?' she asked, bending low to his face, taking his hand in her own. 'And you—you are hurt!'

'I'm done for,' he groaned, 'and so's Heggarty. He's shot, over by the door. Levitt knifed me. Miss, get away! If he finds you—'

'Where are they now?'

'In the kitchen,' he panted, 'they've got the others there, bailed up; they're drinking, and eating, and they mean to take the horses and head north, following the mountains. For God's sake go! Take the stallion!'

His eyes closed; his face suddenly twisted in wrenching pain. Sobbing between her teeth, she lifted him to a sitting position in her strong young arms; his head lolled on her shoulder. She eased him, pillowing him upon her breast; great shudders racked his thin body.

'Oh—how can I help you?' she cried.

His eyelids fluttered open; he looked up into the fair face above him. He gazed into her eyes for a moment. A little smile flickered across his drained and contorted features, and he spoke so faintly that she had to strain to catch his words.

'My Margaret's got eyes like yours,' he said.

He began gasping for breath; in an agony of compassion she rocked him on her breast. A tear fell on his face. He struggled, and through writhing upturned mouth, spoke his final words.

'Tell the master—it was that rat Burton who opened the door for them,' he said. He turned his head on her bosom; gave a long sigh, and so died— a boy who had gone poaching, one moonlit night in far-away Gloucestershire, and would never see England again.

She held him tightly until his body sagged limp in her arms. She lowered him gently to the grass. Hot tears blinded her eyes; they fell on her cheeks, dried, and were succeeded by a cold rage that took possession of her. Kneeling, she stayed motionless, ears strained, to catch every sound. Her hands were red with the murdered boy's blood, the front of her white gown was soaked with it, she did not notice. She crawled to the corner of the blacksmith's shop. Peering round, she saw the kitchen window blazing with light, and heard distant raucous laughter and clinking of bottles. Ten yards of moonlit space separated her from the back of the stables; she covered them in lithe swift strides, and flattened herself against the outer wall. She inched along to the back window of the stable building, and peered through. Her heart leaped as she saw that they had posted no guard on the horses. Fools! Animals! Murderers! She was icy cold now, a quivering sheath of calculating clear-headed fury. She lifted the wooden shutter and slithered through the black aperture into the stable.

David's great stallion, Wildfire, was in his stall. Wildfire showed a white eye as she approached like a shadow over the rough floor. The stallion champed a little, and moved his feet in the straw. But she put a soft hand on his roman nose, and whispered quietly to him, and he stood; for he knew her voice well; she had never ridden him, but they were friends. She had spent many pleasant half-hours talking to him, caressing him, bringing him apples and carrots from the garden. He made no sound as she brought a bridle from the wall and fitted it on him. She held her breath as she slid the bit into his mouth. If he whinnied, heaven help her! But he did not. Still whispering to him, she led him from the stall. One or two of the other horses snickered as she took Wildfire past them; softly, soothingly, she spoke their names.

They reached the door; she slid back the bar; opened it cautiously. The mounting block was a few feet away, obliquely visible from the kitchen. Her skin prickled as she led the horse towards it. Her eyes searched the shadows. If he should spring upon her, before she was safely mounted, then she was lost. But all was silent.

Either Levitt was still vainly searching the house, or had given up for the time being to replenish his supplies of rum in the kitchen.

They gained the block; the horse stood; she jumped on to the flat top of the hewn-off tree trunk, and sprang upon Wildfire's back. David's words, to which she had barely attended at the time, came back to her mind in this moment of need. 'Follow a straight line—past the two beech trees—right-angles to the blacksmith's. You strike a creek—turn right—come to the camp.' She prayed that her memory was not at fault. Why had she not listened more closely! But the chance had to be taken. She must reach David.

She gathered the reins, and eased the stallion, tight-reined, around the corner of the stables. She held his head firmly as he danced past the trees, and through the shadowy grasses. The moments ticked by as they went softly through the patches of light and darkness, working their way quietly towards the edge of the home enclosure; she glanced over her shoulder, to ascertain the direction that they should take; tingling with apprehension, expecting every second that the two of them would be seen, the alarm raised, and she would be pursued. Considering the matter, she thought that if her escape were observed, she could probably outrun them on Wildfire. But then they would get away, long before she could bring back David and the men. And they might escape justice. No; they were going to be caught; and caught red-handed; and pay for their crimes. She, Bethesda Carfax, would see to that.

Still unobserved from the house, they came finally to the edge of the home paddock. With darkness and silence before them, where the empty plains spread wide, she dug her bare heels into the horse's sides and gave him his head.

He took off with a leap that almost threw her.

In later years Bethesda could not remember the details of that ride. She had never even ridden astride, much less bareback. She had never been on Wildfire's back; he was not fully trained; David was gradually preparing him for the winter race meetings. It was a miracle from Heaven that he had not panicked at the smell of the blood on her gown. She uttered a silent and fervent prayer of thankfulness for the many occasions on which she had visited the stallion in his stall, talking, petting and making much of him.

Now, twisting her hands into his mane, she gripped with knees and heels, hanging low on Wildfire's back. As he soared over the homestead fence as though it did not exist, she thought she was surely lost; she rocked and almost fell. Miraculously, she found her balance, clinging like a burr to his withers, then she was lost in the maelstrom of confused and hurrying impressions. The thudding of galloping hoofs, whirling glimpses of stars and sky and trees, beyond Wildfire's great shoulder; his coarse mane whipping her face, though she did not feel the sting of it—her flying tangled hair mingled with his. The swiftness, the power of his mighty stride as they fled away through the night—on and on, through the tall savannah trees, across the rippling expanses of yellow-brown grasses—on and on until her head swam, and dimly, she remembered and held to the thought that she must turn him at the creek.

At length a low line of she-oaks and willows came into view on the flat horizon. These marked the course of the creekbed, and she began to turn the stallion's head, calling to him, reining gently yet imperatively to the right. He had exhausted his first exuberance, and was running at a steady fast canter; he eased his pace slightly, responding to her, and took an oblique course towards the trees; as they approached the banks, he angled obediently, and set off at a steady clip along the direction of the narrow stream.

And so they came, at last, in the still clear night, to the camp. The sound of her approach had alerted the man on watch; and horrified faces surrounded them both; flying into their midst came the horse and the girl—the girl crying out, calling to them, the horse lathered and heaving. She slid, half-falling, from Wildfire's back, sagging against his wet side, one arm hooked over his neck, or else she had fallen to the ground. Soaked with blood and sweat, through chattering teeth she gasped out the story, to the sounds of shouts and running feet; and then slumped into the strong arms that stretched out to her, catching her before she fell.

CHAPTER
ELEVEN

DRIFTING from sleep to dreamy wakefulness and back again, lying among the pillows in her bed at the homestead, Bethesda was but fleetingly aware of anxious faces bending and hovering above her, and of voices speaking quietly, seemingly far off. Surfacing from the hazy depths of semi-consciousness, she recognised the voices; but without feeling any particular interest. To pay attention was too much trouble.

'You are sure she is all right, Clancy?' that was David. 'She seems so exhausted—can there be some hidden injury?'

'No, no,' the housekeeper answered in reassuring tones. 'She's only tired out, sir, and no wonder, after such an ordeal! When I saw the state she was in, after you brought her home, well! I got a fright, indeed! But there's only scratches and bruises, sir; she needs sleep, the more the better; better just to leave her rest, until she wakes.'

The voices faded into a low murmur, as they moved away from the bed. Bethesda suddenly opened her eyes.

'Did they get away?' she said clearly. 'Did you catch them?'

The two turned back in surprise. David smiled.

'So—you are awake!' he exclaimed. 'Yes—we caught

them, my dear, in the act of stealing the horses, before making their escape to the north. They are now on their way to Sydney under heavy guard. They will be tried for murder, and Burton with them—it was he who unfastened the door to them; they had bribed him, before they left. They will hang, for poor Rogers, and for the men they killed on the wagon.'

'Good,' said Bethesda, with satisfaction. She lay back in silence for a moment, and then spoke again.

'Heggarty? Is he dead too? Rogers said—'

'Heggarty will live,' David told her. 'It is happy news indeed. The surgeon extracted the bullet—and the lung seems untouched. He will recover, with careful nursing; Clancy will see to that!'

'Too right I will, sir,' Clancy agreed with fervour. 'But we're all that sorry about young Rogers.'

'Yes,' David said. 'Deeply sorry—and angry too. He was a good lad; I trusted him—and he was due very soon for his ticket-of-leave.'

'He—he had a sweetheart,' Bethesda said huskily. There was a pause. She closed her eyes; her lips trembled; she turned her face into the pillows.

David bent over her, and smoothed her hair with a caressing hand. 'We found a letter from her, among his personal possessions,' he said gently. 'I will write to her, and send her the few small things he owned. We can do no more. He died a man's death, my dear, and here on Bellethorpe his name will be always remembered. Now, you must rest, my brave girl; I will stay with you until you sleep.'

Her eyes remained shut; and a tear slid under the lids and coursed down her white cheek. But presently, in spite of herself, weariness took possession of her body and mind and she began to float away on waves of drowsiness.

'I'll leave her in your charge, Clancy,' David said, turning to the door. 'Send Molly to sit with her; I don't want her to be alone.'

'She's a rare young lady, no doubt about that,' Clancy said, as they moved away. 'And her fresh from England, and not used at all to our rough ways! I don't reckon many young ladies could have done it—ridden all that way in the dark, over strange country, and on a half-broke horse—my word! There wouldn't be too many could do that—and her a raw new-chum, as I say!'

A faint sigh, a thread of a voice, from the bed, arrested them and made them turn their heads. But Bethesda seemed asleep, and made no sound. Even if they had been able to catch the murmured words, they would have been no wiser.

For Bethesda had said:

'Constance would have done it.'

'Miss Carfax,' said David with formal courtesy, across the breakfast table, 'would you care to visit Sydney Town?'

He held a letter in his hand; his brown eyes met hers in a smile.

'I must spend a few days there on business,' he explained. 'I thought you might care to accompany me. Molly could travel with us, to bear you company—you may perhaps like to make some purchases at the bond-store. It might raise your spirits, my dear. You have been a little low of late, I believe.'

It was true. Some weeks had passed since the night of the raid upon the station. The lad Rogers had been laid to rest in a quiet corner of the homestead garden; Heggarty was well on the way to a full recovery from his wound; and life continued on its usual even flow. But Bethesda could not overcome a pervading melancholy. The future seemed to stretch so emptily before her. The ache of longing for home, England, Marcus, did not seem to be lessening, but rather to grow in intensity. She had tried her best to hide her sadness and weariness; but it was difficult to dissemble.

After a moment's hesitation, she said,

'Thank you. I think I should like that. There are indeed one or two things I should buy—and the journey would make a pleasant change. What of the children? Can the school be closed while I am away?'

His eyes twinkled. 'I don't think the children will object to a holiday,' he said. 'And since you have received your salary for the quarter, it seems an appropriate time to visit the town.'

'Yes—thank you,' she repeated, giving him a little smile. 'You are very kind. I shall look forward to it.'

So it came about that some days later, Bethesda found herself installed, with Molly in an adjoining bedchamber, in the inn situated near Circular Quay, handily placed to watch the ever-changing activities of the great blue harbour, or to visit the nearby premises where a surprising variety of imported merchandise was for sale. Browsing through the stands and shelves, with Molly beside her, and a bored Bellethorpe henchman leaning on the doorframe whistling through his teeth, she laid out most of her slender store of money on a new gown of pink calico, and a cheap straw bonnet bound with pink ribbon to go with it. The two girls stood side by side, gazing at a creation just unpacked; a ball-dress of gold and amber silk, trimmed with delicate lace and ruched ribbons of bronze velvet. 'Oh, Miss!' Molly breathed in ecstasy. 'You would look a treat in that!' Looking rather wistfully at the dress Bethesda secretly agreed. The gown would admirably become her; there was only one problem; it was priced at two hundred guineas. Besides —the Viscountess Mainwaring would have worn such a dress; a humble governess on a colonial property had no use for it. She turned away with a little sigh. She did not have two hundred guineas, in any case, for her money, together with her jewels, was far away in England. It did not matter. She would never need such things again.

David appeared suddenly in the entrance of the store.

'I guessed I might find you here,' he said with a grin. 'There is some excitement at the shipping office. A schooner has been sighted off the South Head; from the signals she flies, she is the *Southern Cross*, out from England, under Captain Pierce. Would you like to come down to the wharf and watch her berth? I am going; she may be carrying mail.

Bethesda caught her breath in sudden excitement. A ship—from England—a ship, with people, who had actually come from home! Her eyes lit up, and a tinge of colour ran up under her creamy skin.

'Why, yes!' she answered. 'I would like that! Actually to see a ship from home; to hear the news—what has been happening—how interesting it will be! Let us hurry down, and watch her come in!'

'There is no hurry,' he answered, laughing. 'She won't dock for some hours yet. We will have luncheon first; and then go down and watch, if you like.'

After luncheon, with Molly following behind, they left the inn together, and made their way over the dusty paving stones that comprised the roadway to the quay. The afternoon was bright and clear, and as always, a salt breeze blew in from the harbour, and the blue wavelets danced gleaming in the sun. Bethesda and David found a vantage point, a little removed from the shouting, cursing, bustling, scurrying crowd that milled around them. The heat of the sun was considerable, and Bethesda put up her parasol, as the tall graceful ship was brought in and fastened to her moorings. Passengers with rosy English faces could be seen lining the rail. She understood their bewilderment and their somewhat apprehensive looks. Had she not felt like that herself, a few short months ago! And in actual fact, did she not feel just as unhappy still!

All her unhappy excitement drained away; and the realisation dawned upon her that coming down to see an English ship had been a mistake. It had brought her own intolerable homesickness flooding back with even greater violence. Tears of pain and misery rose to her eyes. Frantically, she bit her lips, and forced the tears back. She could not break down here—in this public place. She moved the parasol slightly, and fixed her gaze on a point to the side, away from sight of the incoming vessel, with its associations of home, love and happiness. David had moved a little aside, and was busy in conversation with a business acquaintance; Molly was engrossed in exchanging winks and saucy looks with a handsome redcoat who lounged close by. Bethesda stood rigid, both hands clenched on the handle of her parasol, teeth gritted together; half turned from the travellers who had begun to descend the gangway. She stared across the brilliant waters, unseeing, her thoughts flying beyond the tangible; hardly aware of heat-waves rising from the ground about her, or the rough paving beneath her feet.

Marcus and his sister came hand-in-hand down the swaying gangplank. They stood close together, looking around. A feeling of unreality held them both; here was journey's end, and yet it seemed as if they had not arrived. The wharf seemed to rock and heave under their feet; once or twice, as they stood, rather at a loss in the midst of the noisy scene, Constance put her hand on her brother's arm to steady herself. The dazzling light, and the blistering heat of the sun, washed over them and enveloped their senses in a luminous haze. Constance, leaning on Marcus's arm, shaded her eyes with one gloved hand, and tried valiantly to marshall her wits.

'Marcus!' she cried out, in sudden fear. 'What if she is not here? What if we cannot find her?'

'She must be here,' he answered grimly, above her head. His eyes were scanning the crowd. 'We will search the whole place; she must be here, Connie!'

Constance began looking at the faces of the hurrying people about them.

She turned her head; and saw, suddenly, a tall young lady in a calico gown, standing apparently alone. The lady held a parasol that obscured her face from Constance's gaze; but something caught the watcher's attention—something half-recognised, familiar, about that figure; and, screwing up her eyes, and squinting through the heat-haze, she saw a bright red curl, across a cotton-clad shoulder. On a sudden impulse, she caught at Marcus's arm; and at the moment, the parasol moved a little—and she saw the lady's profile.

It was Bethesda.

There was a moment of shock, of rigidity; they seemed suspended in time.

Then Lady Constance, daughter of a line of belted Earls, schooled from birth in the correct behaviour required of a great lady—which included never giving vent to one's feelings in public, no matter what the provocation—opened her mouth to its uttermost, and screamed.

She screamed louder than any fishwife ever did, at dawn, in full cry at Billingsgate markets.

'Bethy!' shrieked Constance. 'Bethy—Bethy— Bethy!'

Her voice cut shrilly through the bustle and noise. Bethesda turned her head. She heard Constance cry out; saw her running, pushing through the crowd; looked straight into her face.

The parasol fell from Bethesda's hands. The world swung dizzily about her. Blackness rushed over her; and she slumped to the ground.

David, looking around, saw her sway, and moved quickly toward her.

But it was Marcus, running hard on Constance's heels, who covered the intervening distance in a bound, and lifted her in his arms.

Through the rushing in her ears, she was dimly aware of iron arms that caught her up and lifted her; of her head falling forward on to his shoulder; and then she knew no more.

Amid some confusion and curious stares, she was carried over the cobblestones and back to the cool dark inn; laid gently down on an oak settle, as lightly as though she were a feather. She came up from the depths, to hear a voice above her head, as he crushed her to his hard chest, laughing, chiding, sobbing, all at once.

'You little fool! My love—my darling! How dare you leave me! I won't have it, do you hear! Bethy, Bethy! My love, my darling! You shall never do so again!'

It was too much joy; she could not speak; she could only bury her face in his breast, and with her free arm, return the warm embrace of Constance, who half-lay on her shoulder, from the other side. And so they remained, the three of them, lost in a communication too deep for words.

None of them had noticed that David, quietly watching the scene from just inside the tavern door, was standing like a man in a dream, unable to wrench his eyes away from the tender blue eyes, the soft gentle mouth, the sweet wild-rose face of Constance, as she leaned in a passion of yearning over her lost friend. Constance had cast her bonnet upon the floor; her shining pale-brown hair was banded around her small head; her little neck was white as swansdown; she would stand no higher than his heart.

David Aubyn gazed like a man bewitched.

He had seen the one—the only woman. He did not even know her name. But he knew her, for all that.

It was several hours later.

The remains of their dinner had been cleared away, but the four young people still sat on at the table, in the candlelight, in the low-beamed parlour of the inn.

The long story had been told and re-told; there were no more secrets to be revealed; and now they sat in comfortable silence. Marcus's arm encircled his wife's waist; her hand was clasped in his; her head rested snugly upon his shoulder. In a happy dream, she leaned against him, smiling mistily at Constance, who sat opposite, with David beside her. She thought, almost, she must be still dreaming, and would wake, as she so often had, with Marcus's name on her lips, and her heart bleeding, in her narrow bed at Bellethorpe. She reached across the table to Constance; her hand was taken, held—no, no, it was no dream, but true, miraculous reality. Constance was not dead. Marcus was here beside her. All was well, and soon they would return, all three of them, to home, to England; and life would be as it always had. She gave a great sigh of happiness.

CHAPTER
TWELVE

'MARCUS,' Bethesda said, entering the Bellethorpe breakfast-parlour from the verandah door, her straw hat hanging by its ribbons down her back, 'Marcus, have you seen Connie anywhere? She's not in her room, nor in the garden either.'

'Gone riding with Aubyn,' Marcus replied, looking up from his scrutiny of a journal that lay open on the table. 'I say, Bethy; this newspaper—it's almost a year old!'

'Of course it is; the papers have to come by ship,' said his wife. 'But—Marcus—did you say—Connie out riding alone with David? Ought she to be—'

'Oh, she's quite safe with him,' answered Marcus easily, flicking over the pages. 'As a matter of fact, Bethy—I've been meaning to—' he stopped, and seemed on the point of adding some further remark; but the sound of approaching hooves was heard, cantering along the gravel driveway. In a very few minutes, voices and laughter heralded the return of the truants. The door opened, to admit Constance, flushed and glowing, followed by David.

'I thought you had no equal as a horsewoman, Bethesda,' he declared, laughing, 'but now—I would not care to be the judge! Having watched Lady Constance take Merrilees over the bottom fence—my heart was in my mouth, Mainwaring, and I swear to you I had no notion she meant to do it—!'

'I ain't surprised,' said Marcus, grinning, 'and it's only a matter of time before she inveigles you into letting her mount Wildfire. She and Bethy are as bruising a pair of riders as I ever saw; they've both followed the hunt since they were infants.'

'I can well believe it,' responded David; and his eyes rested upon Constance with a look of love and pride.

'Why, Connie, love!' Bethesda said, 'Where did you find a riding dress? You brought none with you, surely?'

There was a tiny pause. Constance blushed sweetly; and lifted her face to David's.

'It—it belonged to Mrs Aubyn—to David's Mama,' she answered. 'David—Mr Aubyn—thought that it would fit me.'

'And so it does,' said David warmly, 'and becomes you mightily, too.'

Ther was a short silence. Marcus appeared to be absorbed in some item of interest in the year-old journal. Bethesda, staring in some surprise at the two people before her, was suddenly assailed by a terrible suspicion. She dismissed it instantly; it was impossible; not to be thought of. At that moment, the door opened to admit Molly and Mistress Clancy, bearing breakfast trays of home-cured bacon, eggs, and the enormous white tea-pot that gushed forth the strong black fluid which David called tea. This inky potion was quite unrelated to the straw-coloured liquid sipped from fluted cups in English drawing-rooms. One taste of it had set Bethesda shuddering; she was surprised again to see that Constance accepted a steaming cup, and sipped the vulgar brew with every sign of enjoyment, her blue eyes laughing at David above the thick china rim.

The *Southern Cross* was due out from Sydney Town in four weeks' time. Their return passages were booked. The fortnight just gone by had been passed pleasantly enough at Bellethorpe, though Bethesda found the blistering heat hard to bear, and longed constantly for the damp cold scent of autumn, falling leaves, the rains that would be misting even now across the moors; the smell of the salt winds curling in from the north, precursors of the wild gales of winter so soon to follow.

Sitting in the drawing-room during the evening, fanning herself rather listlessly, Bethesda glanced across at Constance, who was idly turning the pages of an old album, and humming the tunes to her own accompaniment on the pianoforte. Bethesda said, sighing,

'Oh, Connie, how I long to be home! To be at Ribston again, with snow on the outcrops, and sleet hissing past the windows! This heat—! Don't you find it trying? I declare, love, I never even imagined a place such as this. Oh—to gallop over the high moors, with the rain on my face!'

There was a short silence. Constance sat still, face averted, hands resting on the keys. At last she said, with some hesitation,

'I—I like the warmth. You know, love, I've never liked cold wild weather, as you do. I find the sun and the bright light all around strange, but—but rather wonderful. I—actually, I like it here, very much.'

Bethesda sat up and stared, incredulous.

'You like it—this rough, awful place? Connie, you can't!'

'But I do,' said Constance resolutely. 'I enjoy the silence, and the space, and the wilderness and strangeness. I feel—at home here, Bethy.'

Stunned into silence, her eyes fixed on Constance's profile, Bethesda was all at once revisited by the incredible, the awful suspicion that had leaped into her brain that morning in the breakfast-parlour.

'Connie!' she exclaimed, in a stifled voice. 'You are not—you haven't—you couldn't—'

Constance slid from the paino stool, darted across the room, and threw herself into her friend's arms.

'Oh, Bethy! I am so happy!' she cried, her voice muffled against the lace of Bethesda's breast. 'I love him so! He has asked Marcus for my hand in marriage; they are talking about it now! Didn't you wonder why they are so long together in the bookroom? Oh, love, wish me happy!'

Torn by conflicting emotions, Bethesda held the slight body close to her. The thought of separation from Constance appalled and horrified her. So small, so tenderly nurtured, cradled in luxury since her birth; how could she survive if she stayed here? A brilliant marriage, a life of elegance, with every possible comfort, was Constance's appointed destiny. Not the rigours of living in this awful place! And the distance—she would be so far away—why, they might never meet again!

Anguished words of protest rose to Bethesda's lips. But she could not utter them.

For Connie loved him. And that she understood.

She looked down at the childish head resting on her shoulder; and gave one long quivering sigh.

The door opened. Marcus and David stood on the threshold.

'Bethy, we have some news for you,' said Marcus gently.

'She knows!' cried Constance, lifting her head. 'Bethy

knows; and she wishes us both happy.' She jumped to her feet, and quickly crossed the room, to stand beside her man, head proudly held, blue eyes glowing. She took David's brown hand in her own, and lifted it to her face, before he imprisoned it in both of his own.

'I am the luckiest man alive,' he said. 'I will take care of her; she shall be first in my life, always. You have my word on that, Marcus.'

'I know it,' the Viscount responded. 'Bethy, what do you say?'

Her immediate impulse was to weep. But somehow, she summoned a smile; swept gracefully forward, and kissed them both tenderly.

'You will be so happy together, I know,' she said. 'You and I will be brother and sister, David. What do you think of that?'

'I am doubly fortunate,' he answered sincerely, with a direct look from his frank brown eyes. 'For I was often used to think, my dear, that had I been blessed with a sister, I should have wished her to be just like you.'

Late that evening, alone with her husband, Bethesda said forlornly,

'Marcus, I still feel quite overwhelmed. The mere thought of leaving Connie here is too much for me to bear. Are you sure, love? Are you quite sure that David is the man for her? She has known him scarce a fortnight, remember!'

'And do you remember walking down a staircase— and I saw you?' demanded the Viscount. 'It was so with us, was it not? A fortnight is long enough; or a day—or an hour.'

After a short but satisfactory interlude, Bethesda

spoke again, her voice somewhat stifled, as was to be expected, as her face was pressed against his chest.

'But, Marcus, have you thought—have you considered how Connie will be, living here? She will soon grow old, in this terrible sun; her looks will fade—she will be brown, and lined, and freckled, like the others I have seen . . . and she will have none of the luxury that is hers by right, that she is used to—none of the elegancy of society. And—and, Marcus, she is so small, so fragile—'

'She will be always beautiful in Aubyn's eyes,' Marcus said firmly. 'And as for being fragile, Bethy, no such thing! Connie looks as if a strong wind would blow her away; always did; but she ain't delicate, not in the least. Quite the opposite! Look how fast she recovered from the accident! Over it in no time, faster than a man. No, no, she's not weak, love, but as strong as a willow wand!'

'But—' his wife sighed. 'But, Marcus, I still cannot feel that it is right for her. I don't really understand how you came to give your consent.'

Her husband gave her a little shake, and tilted her face up to meet his eyes.

'Now, listen to me, my girl,' he said sternly. 'I am well pleased with this match. Aubyn's a damn good man, a gentleman, a man to be trusted. Think for a minute, love! Think of his care for yourself! When I consider what might have become of you, flying off like that, you little fool—' here followed another brief but delightful interval—'Well, anyway, he's a first-rate chap, and though it's not a brilliant marriage, his birth is unexceptionable. I was at Eton myself with one of his cousins. Connie will be mistress of a large property, and a lady of standing in the colony.' He stopped for a minute, and they were both silent, wrapped in a close embrace. He spoke again.

'And there's another thing, love. You know Connie—how loyal she is, how true. Once she gives her heart, it is forever. What if she gave it to some no-good fortune-hunter, in her first London season, and determined to marry him? Or married some two-faced schemer, just after her fortune, who would spend her wealth on his pleasures, and break her heart? No; she's found a man here who's worthy of her—top-of-the-trees; he'll always care for her; she'll be safe, and happy with him.'

'But we will never see her again!' Bethesda burst out.

'Not very often—and I feel the grief of parting with her already, love, as you do. But David has promised to bring her home every few years. The sailing ships will soon have the voyage time to England down to three months. Think of that, Bethy! Only three months separating this place from home! It is hard to comprehend such speed. But we will all meet, now and then; and I tell you what, love, I think Connie will enjoy living here. I think she will find it quite an exciting and interesting life.'

'Why—Marcus!' Bethesda said in surprise, lifting her face to look into his eyes. 'My lord! Confess! You are enjoying it here yourself!'

For a moment, he grinned like a mischievous school-boy.

'Well . . .' he admitted, 'I am glad I saw this place, Bethy. It's so big—so empty—so much still to be explored. I have a feeling, love, that New South Wales won't always be just a penal colony.'

'Yes,' she agreed, after a moment's thought. 'Yes—I believe you are right.'

And so Bellethorpe woke to its very first wedding day.

A brilliant and lovely day it was. Not a cloud marred the blue of the arching sky; and though summer was now marching across the plains, and the earth turning brown in the heat haze that shimmered in front of the distant mountains, by some merciful dispensation a cool fresh breeze wafted across Bellethorpe on Constance's wedding morning. Long trestle tables, covered with stiff-starched white cloths, were laid out in the shade of the trees that studded the front lawn. The front verandah was garlanded and wreathed in flowers—fragrant bunches from the homestead garden, and bundles of fresh blossoms brought by neighbours, together with trails of greenery, to adorn the pillars and the wide steps, and create a perfumed and lovely setting for the ceremony.

The sprawling homestead was jammed to the rafters; the entire colony seemed to be there. The kitchen buzzed with feverish activity for days before. Mrs Clancy, assisted by the small army of servants who had accompanied their various employers to Bellethorpe, hurried tirelessly back and forth; supervising the baking; the broiling; the roasting; the endless stream of cakes, sweets, and puddings—for the guests had hearty appetites; and thirsts to match. The day before the wedding an impromptu race meeting was held, and certain sporting gentlemen of the district backed their favourites to the tune of quite a few guineas; only to watch Aubyn's Wildfire carry off the honours of the day. However, they paid up with good grace, and refreshed by a hearty dinner and copious libations to go with it, the assembled ladies and gentlemen then proceeded to dance the night hours away in the great shearing-shed, to the strains of fiddle and concertina, until streaks of dawn broke on the horizon. Some of the ladies then retired, to snatch a couple of hours' sleep; some of the gentlemen stretched out under the trees, for the same purpose. But most did not bother to go to sleep at all. Instead, they revived themselves with plentiful draughts of ale laced with rum, and set about the business of jumping their respective horses over the six-barred gate into the home paddock— to the tune of some lively interchanges between rival factions, and some brisk off-course betting on the side.

Even Marcus, accustomed to the fast pace and late hours of London society, was impressed by the endurance of these redoubtable colonials. Bethesda began to express doubts as to whether any of their guests would be still on their feet when the time came for the wedding to be held.

Yet at the appointed hour, a decorous and well-dressed crowd, brushed and pomaded, frilled and furbelowed, the ladies wearing delicate London-made gowns, and several of them sporting jewels that made Bethesda blink, assembled on the lawns before the homestead. Dignified, clothed in sobriety and elegance, they stood awaiting the arrival of the bride. The guests were flanked on either side by the station people, and the visiting servants, all dressed in their best. Heggarty sported a nosegay of flowers in his lapel. Molly had crowned herself with a circlet of roses in honour of the occasion. Mrs Clancy, her face moist and pink as a cabbage rose, beamed beside them. A gargantuan feast was ready in the kitchen, awaiting the signal for the dishes to be carried out. The tables were set, with fine glass and silver; a long table for the servants was there too, beside the others; for by David's orders, master and man, mistress and maid would eat together at his wedding breakfast. And so it was to be, that day, and in the future, at all the weddings which down the long years would be held on the broad lawns of the Aubyn homestead.

Presently, the strains of the wedding march were heard; rendered with great energy on the pianoforte, by a lively young lady from a property some fifty miles distant.

Constance, leaning on the Viscount's arm, appeared from within the house. Her simple white dress had been made by a local seamstress, with the assistance of Mrs Clancy. Her filmy long veil had belonged to David's mother. She wore no jewels, since she had brought none with her on her journey to New South Wales. A crown of white rosebuds circled her shining brown head, and she carried more roses in her hands. Her blue eyes shone; and somehow, she seemed half-luminous, misty; like something from a dream, fair as a flower, and sweet as the buds she wore. Behind her, the Viscountess was a resplendent matron-of-honour, in the amber gown that had taken her eye in Sydney town, and the wonderful betrothal ring that Marcus had replaced upon her hand.

A hush fell over the company. The clergyman, imported at great expense from Sydney Town for the occasion, stepped forward; and the ceremony began.

And so Constance was married.

Lying in her husband's arms, as the *Southern Cross* bore them home to England, Bethesda wept again for the pain of leaving their sister behind. But she knew, in her heart, that it had to be so. Marcus and Bethesda—David and Constance; they belonged, they were a part of a whole. Time, space, distance—nothing could change that; so it must always be.

As the weeks slipped by, drawing them ever closer to home, she suffered many qualms at the prospect of the shock and consternation that awaited their arrival without Constance. She could not feel that either Lady Cumnor or her lord would accept their daughter's marriage with equanimity. They would consider Constance lost to them. Bethesda doubted very much whether they would be able to imagine any possible circumstances in which Constance would have willingly chosen to remain in New South Wales. She became increasingly uneasy, as the voyage progressed, and began almost to dread the day of their landing on English soil.

Voicing these anxious fears to Marcus, however, she was a little reassured by his more optimistic view.

'Mama will come about,' he comforted her. 'I will explain matters to her, and then she'll twist m'father around her thumb; she always does. Besides,' he pointed out with considerable shrewdness, 'Mama's a sensible woman. It ain't as if Connie was an only daughter. Mama's got others.'

'Marcus—!' cried his wife, shocked and outraged. 'How can you say such a dreadful thing! As if your Mama would even think of such a thing!'

'You'll see. Once I convince her that Connie is happy and well established, that's how she will feel. I promise you I'm right, love.'

And so it proved. At first, Lady Cumnor's agitation was extreme. But Marcus was able to reassure her that this strange marriage was in fact right for his sister. And after a time of thoughtful reflection, and a twinge of regret for the loss of her daughter, Lady Cumnor came to accept the situation. She could not entirely like the prospect of prolonged years of separation from Constance. But as her son had pointed out, she was a sensible and practical woman; and she had, after all, three other daughters. Lady Julia, the eldest, was satisfactorily established in matrimony with a doting and affluent baronet. But the younger ones, Caroline and Diana, had still to be successfully launched upon the marriage market; and Caroline was fast approaching her teens. So, the Countess resigned herself to the extraordinary fate of her second daughter; and made the best of things.

Lord and Lady Mainwaring returned to their place in English society, where every indulgence of wealth and adulation were theirs. They remained unfashionably true lovers, as the years flowed past; and in the course of time when Marcus succeeded to his father's estates, he became a forward-thinking and enlightened landlord, concerned with the welfare of his people and of his extensive properties. They always enjoyed the London season, of course, and for many years, the incomparable Countess of Cumnor was the reigning beauty of the ton. But their hearts were drawn to the wild seclusion of Ribston, and they spent as much of their time as was possible on this, the best-loved of all their estates.

Lady Constance had nine years of happiness with her husband. Then David Aubyn was killed in an accident on the station. Despite the fervent entreaties of her family that she should return to England—for she was but twenty-five years old—Constance was adamant; she would never leave Bellethorpe. Supported and advised by her loyal friends the Hobys, and with Heggarty and Clancy at her back, she gathered the reins of management into her small capable hands; and announced her intention of keeping the property safe, until her son should grow to manhood, and take possession of his father's heritage. As the years went by, she received many proposals of marriage. But she had given her heart once and for all, and she never married again. She remained in the colony for the rest of her days, small and sun-dried, active as a little brown sparrow; widely known throughout the settlement as the Grand Old Lady of Bellethorpe. Under her firm and kindly hand, the small school on the station continued and flourished; and she was delighted when a currency lass who had been educated at the Bellethorpe school was appointed as the lady teacher in charge of the first State school to be opened in the district. And when at last, Connie's days were done, she followed the firelight to where David awaited her, and was laid to rest beside him in the tiny Aubyn graveyard behind the homestead.

Just twenty years after that first Bellethorpe wedding, the daughter of David and Constance—a vivid laughing girl with her father's black curls—was married to her childhood sweetheart; her brother's best friend; young Hoby of Redmond. This tall brown lad with steady eyes was the same baby boy whose birth had been gladly announced on the day that Bethesda had arrived at the homestead. Constance watched the young people with joy and pride; and as she looked at them, the thought grew upon her that David was there too, with her, beaming upon these beautiful children as they were married. If she turned her head, Constance thought, she would surely see his beloved face. And she sighed, and wept a quiet tear, and smiled warmly upon the assembled company; and thought what a truly lucky woman she was.

The links between the two families remained strong. In course of time, Bethesda's second son set sail, with his parents' blessing, to join his colonial cousins. He struck out to the north, in the path of the Overlanders, and took up land in the new state of Queensland.

The daughters of Marcus and Bethesda became the famous Mainwaring twins; the Ladies Eustacia and Lucienne. These shimmering blondes were endowed with a double measure of outrageous charm and irrepressible high spirits. They exploded upon the staid mid-Victorian erea like a couple of blazing comets, after which they proceeded to raise every eyebrow in the town, and to set the whole of that ultra-prim and decorous society by the ears.

But that is a story for another day . . .

How to join in a whole new world of romance

It's very easy to subscribe to the Mills & Boon Reader Service. As a regular reader, you can enjoy a whole range of special benefits. Bargain offers. Big cash savings. Your own free Reader Service newsletter, packed with knitting patterns, recipes, competitions, and exclusive book offers.

We send you the very latest titles each month, postage and packing free – no hidden extra charges. There's absolutely no commitment – you receive books for only as long as you want.

We'll send you details. Simply send the coupon – or drop us a line for details about the Mills & Boon Reader Service Subscription Scheme. Post to: Mills & Boon Reader Service, P.O. Box 236, Thornton Road, Croydon, Surrey CR9 3RU, England. *Please note: READERS IN SOUTH AFRICA please write to: Mills & Boon Reader Service of Southern Africa, Private Bag X3010, Randburg 2125, S. Africa.

Please send me details of the Mills & Boon Subscription Scheme.

NAME (Mrs/Miss) _____ EP3

ADDRESS _____

COUNTY/COUNTRY_____ POST/ZIP CODE_____

BLOCK LETTERS, PLEASE

Mills & Boon
the rose of romance